Relentless

By

Eve Vaughn

Dedication

Wanda, you have been such a huge help and inspiration to me this year with your words of encouragement and ear to listen to whenever I want to vent. I don't know what I'd do without you. Thank you for being an awesome friend.

To my inspiration keep writing, my family who builds me up and keeps me going. I love you all.

"I'm going to break you. And I'm going to make you love every second of it."

Enemies at first sight...

Displaced from her home and dealing with the loss of a loved one, Krystina Jackson is met with a hostile force in the form of Dominic Holden. She clashes with him on every turn until she decides avoidance is the best solution.

An inconvenient attraction...

From the second Dominic laid eyes on Krystina she managed to get under his skin and not in a good way. For reasons of his own, he's determined to keep her at arm's length. However, when the irritating little girl turns into an appealing woman, Dominic is forced to reassess his feelings.

An obsession is born...

Determined to get Krystina out of his system, Dominic sets forth a plan to conquer her and bend her to his will by any means necessary. But as his plot plays out, he may soon find himself snared in a web of his own making.

Chapter One

"You don't belong here. You never will."

"Ms. Jackson?"

Krystina jerked to attention when a hand fell on her shoulder bringing her out of her deep musings. She turned to see an older gentleman in a dark suit holding a sign in his hand with her name on it. Raising a brow in surprise, she took a cautious step backward. "Yes?"

"I'm Douglas, your driver, here to take you to your destination."

She furrowed her brow in confusion. "Uh, I didn't order a car service. I'd planned to catch a cab."

"There's no need for that ma'am. It's all been arranged. Mr. Holden's instructions."

A slight smile touched her lips. For the first time since she'd stepped off the plane, her already elevated anxiety slightly abated. Uncle Charles was a thoughtful man. It was kind of him to arrange transportation for her. "Oh, well, in that case, thank you."

"Let me help you with your bags. Is this all?" Douglas looked at her carry-on and large suitcase.

She nodded. "Yes, thank you. You can take the big one. I can handle the other."

"It would be no problem for me to take both."

"Really, I don't mind." Krystina rolled the larger of the two cases toward the driver. "Lead the way."

Douglas took the bag. "Follow me."

Once Krystina's luggage was in the trunk and she was ensconced within the back of the luxury vehicle, her thoughts began to drift to memories best buried in the past. During her lengthy flight from Paris, she'd tried to keep her mind occupied, focusing on this new chapter in her life. If she could just make it past the next several weeks, or at least however long it took her to find suitable accommodations she'd be all set.

Her carefully laid out plans had taken a slight detour when her old college roommate who she'd planned to room with had gotten engaged. Stella had decided that it made financial sense for her and her fiancé to move in together sooner rather than later.

Krystina understood but it had put her in a sticky situation, which was why she was now headed to the one place she said, she'd never step foot in again. If it weren't for Uncle Charles, she certainly wouldn't have but after all he'd done for her, she could hardly turn down his invitation without seeming ungrateful.

Releasing a heavy sigh, she leaned her head back against the leather upholstery and closed her eyes.

"We'll be living here?" Krystina eyed the massive estate with wonder. She'd only seen homes like this on television. What stood before her in all its opposing glory was a pure architectural masterpiece with its imposing columns on the porch and huge circular driveway with a fountain in the middle. The massive manicured lawn probably could have fit the entire block of her old neighborhood and then some. It never occurred to her that people outside of Hollywood or those who weren't royalty actually lived like this. It was a far cry from the rickety old house she'd shared with her grandmother in a backwoods Mississippi town that had been devastated by a

8

natural disaster. Only a few weeks ago, they had been homeless. Krystina had never expected anything so fancy.

"Close your mouth girl before a fly lands in there."

Krystina promptly shut her lips despite the fact that the windows were rolled up and there was no chance of any insects getting in. She knew better than to talk back to the older woman who never hesitated in doling out a little corporal punishment.

Once the driver parked the vehicle in a carport that held several cars, he led them to a side entrance. The inside of the house was even grander than she imagined it would be with its double spiraling staircases, vaulted ceilings and giant chandelier. She gasped in awe. Everything looked so expensive that she was too scared to touch anything and if she really wanted to.

A tall, thin woman with iron gray hair and an unreadable expression approached them after the driver who'd escorted them in had disappeared. "I'm Ms. Lakes, the estate manager. Jeffrey will take your things to your rooms. In the meantime, I'll show you to the living room where you can make yourselves comfortable, although I caution you to be very careful in there because there are many valuable items we'd rather not see damaged." She offered a tight smile before turning on her heel and walking away. Krystina's grandmother let out a soft 'humph' before taking her hand and following the woman.

Even in Krystina's eleven-year-old mind, she'd understood the insult in Ms. Lakes words, as if they would destroy property when they'd barely gotten inside the house. After taking their seats, the estate manager gave them a smile that didn't quite reach her eyes. "So, Willie Mae is it? Didn't you use to be the Holden's maid? How generous of them to take you and your granddaughter in after that unfortunate incident."

Krystina narrowed her eyes. Already, she disliked this woman. Where she came from no one used an elder's first name unless given permission and even though Ms. Lakes was up there in years, Krystina was certain Grandma had her beat. "It's Miss Jackson," she piped up.

Ms. Lakes raised a brow. "Oh, my apologies. I figured you'd be back in a domestic capacity so...of course. Forgive my lapse of judgment. I'll inform Mr. Holden you've arrived. In the meantime, I'll have a maid see to it that you get refreshments."

As soon as the woman was out of the room, Grandma pursed her lips. "I don't trust that heifer for as far as I can throw her. When I worked here, we didn't need all these servants for so few people. Estate manager, my foot."

Krystina simply nodded in agreement.

"But, I taught you better than that. You don't put your nose in grown folks' conversation."

"Sorry."

Grandma sighed. "It's okay this time but watch that mouth. It will get you in trouble one day. Don't end up like your mother."

It was on the tip of Krystina's tongue to give a smart retort but she'd been on the receiving end of her grandmother's backhand before and didn't wish to experience it now. She bit the inside of her bottom lip, hating that once again her mother's sins were thrown in her face. She couldn't help what her mother had done but it seemed like she was constantly paying for it. There were times when Krystina wondered if her grandmother actually thought she was her mother. Sometimes Grandma would call Krystina by her mother's name. It had become a more frequent occurrence since Candice Jackson's death two years ago.

"I'm not her," Krystina muttered under her breath.

"What did you say?" Grandma asked with a raised brow and folded arms.

"Nothing."

"Yeah, that's what I thought."

Krystina folded her hands in her lap and bowed her head. She had no doubt that her grandmother cared about her, but lately, Grandma had been short-tempered and the smallest thing seemed to set her off. Krystina tried to be understanding, after all, the last several weeks had been stressful. They'd survived a major disaster, and in the process lost several neighbors and close friends. Krystina shuddered as she thought of the bodies she'd seen floating by their house, some of whom she'd known most of her life. During the harrowing days when she wasn't sure what their fate would be, Krystina had nearly lost her grandmother. It was probably something that weighed heavily on Grandma's mind as well.

Krystina was so lost in thought that she didn't notice another person enter the room. She felt the heated stare before she actually saw it. When Krystina raised her head, her gaze collided with a pair of eyes that were somewhere between the color of blue and green. They were so clear and vibrant that in other circumstances she might have been impressed but what immediately struck her was the hostility lurking within that haughty look. The boy…no, he was too old to be called that but he didn't quite look old enough to be labeled a man, frowned in her direction. His lip was slightly curled into a sneer as if what he saw before him was not to his liking.

She didn't know who he was and frankly, she didn't care, but this person didn't get to look down at her like she was trash. She didn't ask to be here and if their house hadn't been destroyed, Krystina would have gladly gone back to Mississippi. Refusing to be intimidated, she narrowed her eyes and glared back at him.

Grandma was the first to speak. "Well, if it isn't Little Dom. Look at you. You're so tall and handsome. I ain't seen you since you were still a child. Come hug my neck." With no little effort, she got off the couch to stand.

Little Dom as Grandma had referred to him seemed reluctant to comply but finally walked over to the older woman *and gave her a half-hearted hug. "Hello, Miss Jackson." He immediately took a few steps back when he was finished. "I, uh, prefer to be called Dominic now. No one has used Little Dom in years."*

"Oh," Grandma paused. "Well, it's good seeing you. Are you in school?"

He nodded. "Yes, ma'am. I'm a sophomore at Columbia. We're on break right now and I'll be going back in a couple weeks."

"Good. I know your Granddaddy must be proud."

He offered a tight smile in return. It was quite obvious that he would rather be somewhere else. Every so often, he would shoot a hostile stare in Krystina's direction. Grandma must have noticed as well because she placed her hand on Krystina's shoulder. "This is my grandbaby Krystina."

Instead of even the pretense of a greeting, he stared blankly at her as if he didn't like what he saw. "If you'll excuse me, I have to meet up with a few friends. Uh…nice seeing you again, Mrs. Jackson." He turned on his heel and walked out the room without a backward glance.

"I don't like him," Krystina muttered.

"Well, it doesn't matter if you like him or not. His grandfather is letting us stay here out of the kindness of his heart. Just keep out of his way while he's here and in a couple weeks he'll be back in school and you won't have to worry about him. He's probably just having a bad day. Pay him no mind."

Krystina had done as her grandmother had said and put it off as a bad day. That moment, however, had set a precedent with them. From the day she had stepped foot in that house, Dominic Holden had been a constant thorn in her side. He made no qualms about letting Krystina know by word or deed, that she wasn't welcome and he would never accept her presence.

"Ms. Jackson, we're here."

Krystina had been so lost in thought that she didn't realize the car was no longer in motion. It had been two full years since she'd stepped foot on this estate and seeing the house again sent a shiver racing up her spine.

"Are you okay, ma'am?" Douglas stood by her now open door, waiting for her to get out.

"Oh, I'm sorry, it's just been a while since I've been here. This place hasn't changed a bit." She slid out of the car, wishing she didn't feel like that insecure ten-year-old again. "Let me help you with the bags."

"That's okay. I can handle them."

"At least, let me get this small one. I probably should have kept it with me in the first place." She reached into the truck, pulling out the carrying case that contained her camera. Krystina rarely let it get out of her sight when she was traveling and probably wouldn't have allowed it to be placed with the rest of her luggage had she not been so distracted.

Once she had her bag firmly in hand, she took a deep breath and squared her shoulders before heading toward the house. Once inside, she was surprised to see a few subtle changes to the décor. Some of the furniture was different and decorations had been rearranged. The hand-painted 24x36 portrait of Charles Holden in a gold frame was still in the same spot she remembered, on the center of the wall in the foyer. Beneath it was a cherry wood table with four 5x7 portraits. There were new additions. As she stepped closer to examine them, she noticed the first two were of Felix and Poppy. She hadn't seen either of them since she'd left New York even though they had exchanged emails over the past three years.

The next picture was of the devil himself, Dominic Holden, her nemesis. He'd caused her so much grief over the years that if she didn't see him for fifty years, that would still be too soon. From the moment she'd arrived with her grandmother, he'd gone out of his way to make her feel unwelcome, by his words and deeds. It got so bad at one point that Charles had taken notice and intervened. After that Dominic was more subtle in letting her know that she didn't belong, by throwing an icy look in her direction or simply giving her the cold shoulder. The final straw came three years ago when he'd crossed a line that even Krystina didn't think he was capable of.

She balled her fists at her sides to keep herself from punching the picture frame with his smug face in the center as she was assaulted by the memories she'd fought to keep under lock and key.

"I don't know what you were thinking to sneak out like that. You're lucky nothing serious happened. What if I hadn't been home and then what?" Krystina shuddered as scenarios of what could have happened to the sixteen-year-old ran through her mind. She'd been surprised to get a call from a crying Poppy, asking if Krystina could come pick her up on the other side of town. Krystina usually spent most of her time on campus but Uncle Charles had asked if she could come home for a few days since her school was on break and he rarely got to see her. She and Poppy weren't particularly close as the younger girl hero worshiped her older brother and since Dominic made his dislike of Krystina known, Poppy kept her distance. The teenager wasn't hostile or even mean, just stand-offish. Whenever Krystina tried to bridge the gap between the two of them, Poppy shut her down so Krystina stayed out of her way.

Poppy wiped away the tears streaming down her cheeks and sniffed. "He said he loved me. I-I trusted him!" And with that, she broke into another wave of noisy sobs.

Krystina wasn't sure how to handle this awkward situation. She could empathize with the sixteen-year-old.

Everything seemed so much more intense at that age. With a sigh, she took one hand off the wheel and patted Poppy on the shoulder. "It'll be all right. It's that guy's loss."

"I can't believe he kicked me out of the car when I wouldn't give it up to him. He could have at least drove me home instead of leaving me in a sketchy part of town."

Krystina wanted to roll her eyes. The neighborhood she'd picked the girl up in wasn't too bad but she supposed someone who had been sheltered most of her life would think that. "Well, you're safe now and that's all that matters. And now that you know what a creep this Jeff guy is, you'll think twice about pulling another stunt like that."

Poppy nodded with another sniff.

Krystina returned her hand to the steering wheel as an awkward silence fell between them.

"Krystina?"

"Yes?"

"Thank you."

"No problem."

"I'm sorry."

"For what?"

"I haven't exactly been nice to you over the years I mean...I was just jea — "

Krystina shook her head. "Don't think about it. You were in distress and I'm glad to have helped. But I do wonder why you called me instead of one of your brothers."

"I tried to get a hold of Felix but he wasn't answering and well...you already know I was grounded. Dominic would have killed me. Maybe if we sneak back in the house, he won't notice."

Krystina didn't particularly want to be a part of Poppy's deception, but she figured the girl had gone through enough for the night. "Okay, your secret is safe with me, but don't let this happen again."

"Thank you! You're the best, Krystina, and I promise, I will never give you a hard time again."

This time Krystina did roll her eyes. *"I'll hold you to that."*

When they made it back to the house, they went through the back service entrance because that point of entry was rarely used. Krystina and Poppy, however, were ambushed when they found Dominic waiting for them at the top of the stairs and there was no doubt about it, he looked pissed.

"Dominic!" Poppy squeaked. The poor girl's eyes were as wide as saucers as she started to tremble.

His narrowed aqua gaze landed on Krystina briefly before going to his sister. *"Mind telling me why you were out after you were grounded?"*

Poppy shot Krystina a pleading look. *"I-I...uh..."*

Dominic raised a brow. *"Cat got your tongue? Funny. You always have plenty to say when you want the latest designer bag or some new trinket."*

"Stop picking on the poor girl. Can't you see you're making her nervous?" It was one thing for him to take his anger out on her, she could handle it, but it was clear that Poppy couldn't.

"You stay the hell out of it. Why are you still standing here anyway? This is a family matter."

"Well excuse the hell out of me for trying to help. The truth of the matter is, I asked her to come out with me. Some friends of mine who don't live far from here invited to me to hear some live music at this coffee house and I invited Poppy because she's been cooped up in the house since I arrived."

He flared his nostrils. *"And I'm sure she told you that she's grounded."*

"I was aware of that. I didn't think you were around so – "

"So you thought you could just go off somewhere with my teenage sister in the middle of the night with a bunch of college students, I presume?"

Krystina rolled her eyes heavenward. "Sorry. I wasn't thinking. It won't happen again."

She turned to walk away, having had her fill of this arrogant beast for the night. But apparently, Dominic wasn't finished because he grabbed her by the arm. "You — to your room," he directed his sister.

"But Dom — "

"Now!" he roared.

Poppy scurried away without a backward glance.

He redirected his glare in Krystina's direction. "As for you…" He pulled her along with him down the hall.

Krystina swatted at his arm. "What the hell is wrong with you? Let me go!"

He tightened his grip on her arm as he tugged her to his sitting room. Once inside, he released her and closed the door. "Not until I get an explanation."

"Are you out of your fucking mind to take my sister out to God knows where in the middle of the night with a bunch of strangers? Who the hell do you think you are?"

It was on the tip of her tongue to deny his accusation but Krystina realized that in doing so she'd get Poppy into even more trouble than the poor girl was probably already in. Besides, there wasn't anything Dominic could do to her other than yell.

"I think I'm someone who doesn't have to stand here and let you talk to me any way you please. Now, let me go. I don't owe you shit!"

"You have a foul mouth. You've always been trouble. From the minute you stepped into this house."

She laughed without humor. "That again? You've been saying things to that effect for years, Dominic and frankly, it's getting boring." Using all the strength in her reserve, Krystina managed to yank her arm out of his hold. But when she would have walked away, he swirled her around to face him, this time grabbing both of her arms in his hands.

17

"*Don't you fucking walk away from me!*" His eyes had grown several shades darker and a vein throbbed in the side of his head.

"Take your hands off me. You asked me who the hell I thought I was, but that's what I should be asking you. Who the hell do you think you are? You don't get to manhandle and yell at me like I'm your damn child. I'm twenty years old, not some little kid you can bully. Go run roughshod over one of your family members, but leave me the hell alone."

Krystina couldn't quite put her finger on how or when things had changed, but she now saw something raging within the depths of Dominic's eyes that screamed danger and it made her tremble. She'd seen him angry before but never like this. "Let me go, Dominic." She tried to inject as much calm into her voice as her tattered nerves would allow to diffuse an explosive situation that was threating to go nuclear.

"That's right, Krystina, you're not my family, are you?"

She glared at him. "You've only told me that a million times. I don't know what —" Krystina didn't get a chance to finish her sentence before he crushed her lips beneath his. She froze, unable to move from the utter shock of the moment. This couldn't be real, either that or she had entered some parallel universe. When Dominic snaked his arm around her waist and cupped the back of her head with his other hand, he began to kiss her in earnest.

This was wrong!

She struggled to break his hold but the more she fought the more bruising his kiss became. When she opened her mouth to tell him to stop, Dominic took advantage of her parted lips and pushed his tongue into her mouth. Krystina pressed her hands against his chest to push him away but something happened at that moment. Maybe it was the feel of his beating heart beneath her fingertips or the sensation of his solid pecs pressed against her. It could have been the way his kiss dominated her senses and made her tingle. Perhaps, it was the heat between her *thighs that seemed to spread and pulse throughout her body. Whatever it was, she found herself melting against the solid wall of his chest.*

Her knees wobbled as the kiss went on and on, robbing her of all ability to think coherently. Dominic molded her bottom in his palms, bringing her pelvis flush with his hardness. The feel of his erection against her was like a bucket of ice water being thrown on her. Suddenly, the realization of their actions hit Krystina at full speed. This was Dominic and she hated him!

She pushed him away with all her might, this time managing to put some distance between them. Panting for breath, she glared at Dominic. "You've done some pretty low things but this..." Unshed tears blinded her and she fought to hold them back. "Why do you hate me so much?"

He twisted his lips into a half sneer. "That's the problem. I don't."

"Well, I hate you enough for the both of us." And with that, she ran past him. This time he didn't stop her. As soon as she made it to her room, she grabbed her suitcase out of her closet and started to pack. Krystina was determined to never come back.

Yet, here she was.

Over the past three years, she'd made excuses to Uncle Charles about why she couldn't come for a visit but how could she turn him down now after learning that he hadn't been in the best of health? Krystina noticed she was in the fourth picture. It was her high school senior picture. Surprised to see this addition to the table alongside Dominic, Poppy and Felix's, she reached out and touched it. The one time Charles had asked for a picture of Krystina's to be included with the rest of the family portraits in the foyer, Dominic had objected. Charles had one of the staff place one anyway and it had mysteriously gone missing.

"So the prodigal child returns after all."

19

Krystina nearly jumped out of her skin, startled by the deep baritone that cut through the silence. She whirled around to see Dominic leaning against the wall with his arms crossed and a smirk tilting his lips.

There was something in his eyes that scared her far more than hostility.

It was lust.

Chapter Two

Krystina moistened her lips with the tip of her tongue. It had been three long years since she'd set eyes on this man so there was no reason she should feel this nervous. She'd probably just imagined that look. After all, according to Poppy and Felix's emails, Dominic was never short of female company. She raised chin defiantly, refusing to allow this man to intimidate her although it was difficult not to be when he focused his aqua gaze in her direction.

She'd forgotten how tall he was, well over six feet with an athletic frame that showed he took care of himself. Though he wasn't exactly her favorite person, even she realized what a good-looking man he was, possessing a strong chiseled jaw lined with stubble that gave him a rugged appearance. His wavy dark hair and sinister brows made his already startling eyes stand out even more. There was no doubt that Dominic Holden was a head turner. It was too bad he was an asshole.

A smirk rested on his lips as he gave her a slow perusal. Krystina willed herself to remain still. "Dominic," she acknowledged him stiffly.

He tilted his head forward. "Duchess."

She stiffened. He'd called her that a few times before and she figured it was his way of mocking her because of where she'd come from. "You know my name. Use it." She sighed. She'd only been here ten minutes and already this man had managed to get under her skin. All she wanted to do was go to her room, take a shower and sleep off the jet lag. Krystina sighed. "Look, I don't plan on staying longer that a few months or at least until I can find other living arrangements so can we just agree to be civil when our paths cross? Until then, I'll stay out of your way and you stay out of mine."

Without waiting for a reply, she walked past him and went up the spiral staircase. When she walked into her room, she breathed a sigh of relief to see there hadn't been any major changes to it. It even had the same bedspread from when she left. Thankfully, her bags were already here. The camera bag that she'd had on her shoulder was placed carefully on the nightstand. She kicked off her heels and flopped on the bed with every intention of just meditating to calm her nerves, but instead she found herself drifting off.

A loud banging on the door jerked Krystina awake. Dread filled her. She hoped it wasn't Dominic here to ruin her day even further. With a yawn, she slid off the bed and walked over to the door before answering it cautiously. To her surprise, Felix was on the other side.

Felix was Dominic's younger brother who had mostly kept to himself and didn't say much to anyone. They were never that close when Krystina had first come to live here because he literally didn't say anything to anyone, but as he grew older he was at least cordial. It wasn't until she'd moved on to college did she and Felix begin to speak on a regular basis and had actually become friends. Krystina found him to be quite witty with a killer sense of humor. Felix had quite the eye for fashion, so she was pleased when he'd gained entrance into his dream school, the Fashion Institute of Technology.

Felix appeared to be a whole new person. Gone was the awkward seventeen-year-old who allowed his hair to cover his eyes and always walked with his head down. In place of that gawky teenager was a man who had finally found comfort in his skin. Gone was the face, plagued by acne. In its place was skin as smooth as a baby's bottom. His once black hair was now platinum blond which was swept back into a style that looked casual but probably cost a fortune at a high-end salon. His eyes were blue like his older brother's but Felix's were slightly darker. He was absolutely stunning. "Felix! What happened to you?"

He grinned to revealed teeth no longer wrapped in braces. "Let's just say, I've adjusted my style a little. Dom said you arrived hours ago and I figured you'd eventually come down to have dinner with us but when you didn't I thought I'd come check in on you."

Krystina frowned. "Dinner? It can't be dinner yet. I only arrived maybe twenty minutes ago."

"Try four hours. Didn't you notice it getting dark?"

She glanced at her watch to see she must have slept longer than she'd thought. "Oh, my God. I didn't realize how tired I actually was. I didn't get a lot of sleep on the plane. Why don't you come on in? We can chit chat while I unpack some of my things."

Felix entered the room and took the seat in front of her desk. "So how long are you sticking around?"

She shrugged. "I'm not sure. I hope to be out of here at least within the next three months. I want something closer to Manhattan."

"Why bother trying to find another place to live when you can stay here as long as you'd like? You know Grandpa would love having you around. He's always boasting about your accomplishments."

A smile touched her lips. That was sweet of Uncle Charles. "As tempting as the offer is, you know staying here permanently isn't a good idea. I'd absolutely murder your brother if I had to stay here longer than I had to."

"Believe it or not, Dom has mellowed a lot since you've left. I know the two of you have never really gotten along but if you could just see things from his point of view —"

Krystina held her hand up to cut him off. "Are you kidding me? He went out of his way to make my life miserable. I was a child and he was practically an adult. He has no excuse."

Felix sighed. "I'm just saying, there are some things that you don't know."

"To be quite honest, I don't really care to either. Dominic and I are oil and water. We'll never get along. That's just how it is with some people."

"I don't think —"

"I get it. He's your brother so, of course, you want to defend him, but I'd rather not talk about him right now. I'd rather hear how you're doing at school?"

Felix's face lit up at the change of conversation. "Fantastic, actually. For my final, we have to design three separate looks: casual, sporty and couture. That's what I've been working on morning, noon and night so basically, I've been without a social life for the past month."

"But, you love it don't you?"

Felix grinned with a twinkle in his eyes. "Absolutely! And this summer, I'll intern at The House of Santangelo!"

"Isn't Andres Santangelo one of your favorite designers?"

"Yes. And I'm one of the five interns he chose to work at his company. I know I'm talented but it helps to have connections. Apparently, he frequents the family resorts and Dom may have pulled a few strings for me. I see that look on your face. Before you say anything, I fully intend to work my ass off and prove that he made the right decision in choosing me."

"I wasn't going to say a thing. I've seen your sketches and some of the outfits you threw together out of practically nothing. You deserve your spot," she assured him. "Is Poppy home as well?"

"Yes, she's home for the week like me. Our apartment is being painted so we came home to avoid all the mess." Felix and Poppy shared a place in the trendy Chelsea area while they attended school, Felix at FIT and Poppy at NYU.

They chatted for a bit more while Krystina put away some of her clothing. "Well, that's about all I'm going to unpack for now. I need to hop in the shower for a quick wash, but you can tell everyone to go ahead with dinner. I'm not that hungry anyway."

"Well, at least, come down for dessert. Besides, Grandpa has been dying to see you."

"Oh, I had planned on seeing him when I was done. I figured I'd see him when he's alone so we can catch up."

Felix raised a questioning brow. "You wouldn't by any chance be avoiding my brother, would you?"

"The less I see of that man the better. I'm sure as long as I'm in this house running into Dominic is inevitable."

"He travels a lot so you probably won't have to deal with him that much. But like I said before, he's…different."

"Hmm."

Felix chuckled. "Ok, I can take a hint. See you downstairs."

Even though it had been nice to see Felix again, the conversation had been draining, especially the parts about Dominic. She'd forgotten how Felix and Poppy thought the sun rose and set on him. Krystina realized she'd have to be careful about what she said around them about their hero. She supposed the hostility between her and Dominic was one of the reasons it had taken them time to warm up to her. Her plan for the next few months was to stay out of Dominic's way whenever possible.

Krystina sighed in relief when she stepped into the shower and the spray of the stinging hot water hit her back, reenergizing her. Though she tried to clear her mind and enjoy the fantastic water pressure she had been deprived of in her tiny apartment in Paris, Krystina couldn't stop thinking about what Felix had said about his brother. There was absolutely no way that Dominic had changed. Based on the mockery he'd made of that greeting earlier, he was the same tormentor.

When Krystina was younger, there was a time when she would have accepted an olive branch from him had he shown her any sign of kindness, but the incident that killed any chance of her even liking him as a person came when she was fifteen. It hadn't been easy to make friends at her school. Krystina had been a fish out of water. She still had a thick southern accent and the other kids at the prestigious private school saw her as an outsider. It didn't help that she was one of the few kids of color. Even the teachers looked at her as if she didn't belong.

One day a group of girls sat with her at lunch, but they weren't just any random kids. They were the most popular girls in the school and the fact that they'd singled her out made Krystina suspicious at first, but they all seemed very nice. The leader of the four girl pack had been Nancy Salvatore. They'd all hang out at Nancy's house after school and talk about boys mostly. Krystina had tried her first joint with them and for a while, she really felt like she was fitting in until they decided it would be a good idea to have a sleepover at Krystina's. She'd never had one before and had even been a bit wary of asking Uncle Charles to host one but, of course, he was delighted that she'd have friends over. He'd even made Ms. Lakes make sure all of their needs were taken care of that night much to the older woman's displeasure.

"Truth or dare?" Carrie Waterson asked through a mouthful of popcorn.

"Eww, didn't anyone teach you to not chew with your mouth open?" Emily Barker shuddered. "How low class." She was Krystina's least favorite of the four girls. Emily always had something sly to say, finding ways to get in little digs about Krystina's background. Krystina was so desperate to fit in that she pretended not to notice.

Carrie rolled her eyes. "We don't need another lesson from the manner's police." She turned her green gaze in Krystina's direction. "So which is it? Truth or dare?"

Krystina wasn't interested in doing something stupid such as licking a toilet bowl seat like they'd made Madison do only minutes earlier. The redhead was still gagging from the experience. "Uh, truth."

Nancy groaned. "Booooring! Come on, girl, live a little."

"Truth." Krystina was more firm in her statement when she said it this time around.

Carrie smirked. "Chicken."

Nancy smirked. "I have a good one." The look on the blonde's face sent a chill up Krystina's spine. She was almost certain that nothing good could come from whatever question was on the ringleader's mind. "So...have you ever seen Dominic naked?"

Krystina had been in the middle of taking a sip from her soda can and nearly choked. She coughed, drawing laughter from the other girls in the room. When she was able to catch her breath to speak, she glared in Nancy's direction. "Of course not. Dominic is gross."

"Are you kidding me? Dominic Holden is sexy as hell. How could you live in the same house as him and not want to jump his bones." Carried demanded.

"Well, first of all, he's always traveling so I barely see him and second, I'm only fifteen and third, to reiterate my previous statement: gross."

"Are you fucking blind? Dominic is a God!" Madison squealed.

Krystina could barely keep herself from gagging. Sure, Dominic was an attractive man, but his personality sucked and that killed any possibility of her thinking of him as anything other than someone she needed to avoid.

"Oh, the things I would do to that man if I had the chance." Carrie licked her lips to emphasize her point.

Krystina wanted to hurl. Resisting the urge to tell them exactly how disgusting she thought this line of conversation was, she hopped off the floor and grabbed the nearly empty bowl of popcorn. "Uh, looks like we're running low on snacks. I'm going downstairs for a refill."

Nancy shrugged with a roll of her eyes. "Whatever."

Happy to get away from that line of conversation, she didn't rush to return. Once the popcorn was replenished and drinks were tucked under her arms, she headed upstairs. She nearly stumbled backward when she saw Dominic standing at the top of the stairs. He made no attempt to come down and if she didn't know any better, she would have thought he was waiting for her but that wasn't possible. Dominic despised her as much as she did him. The only time he actively spoke to her *was to either harass her over something insignificant or if he absolutely had to. She didn't know he was home. He'd didn't usually spend his time home on a Friday night.*

When she attempted to bypass him, he blocked her way. "Excuse me," she muttered through clenched teeth.

"You need to tell your friends *to keep it down. Ms. Lakes says you five have been rowdy and causing a disturbance. Just remember there are other people in this house besides you."*

"Ms. Lakes can drop dead." The woman had been a thorn in her side since she started living here. Every little transgression the estate manager thought Krystina was guilty of was reported to Uncle Charles. Luckily for Krystina, Uncle Charles always shrugged off Ms. Lakes complaints so the hag, started going to Dominic.

Dominic shook his head. "You see, that's your problem. You have no respect for anyone and that's why you don't have friends," he delivered with an acidity that made her take a step back.

She refused, however, to let him see that his comment affected her. "If I don't have any friends, then how do you explain those girls you claim I'm being rowdy with?"

He smirked and jerked his thumb in the direction. "Oh, those girls? They're not your friends. They're using you."

Krystina glared at him. "You just can't stand to see me happy, can you? You're such an ass." When she would have moved around him, he placed his hand on her shoulder.

"Don't believe me? Let's find out, shall we?"

Before she realized what was happening, Dominic guided her toward her room but yanked her away from the door before she could enter.

"What are you —"

He placed his finger over his lips to indicate she should be silent. Krystina had every intention of telling him to go to hell, when she heard the girls inside, giggling.

"How much longer do you think we have to hang around that loser?" The voice belonged to Emily.

"I guess for as long as it takes for my father to set something up with her guardian. Apparently, the old man is dragging his feet over a business proposition and daddy thinks if I'm friends with his ward, it may ease the transaction through. Look, I'm not exactly thrilled to hang out with her either but Daddy promised me the beamer I wanted for my birthday." Nancy replied.

"All this for a car? Is it really worth it?" Carrie asked. "I mean, this girl is no fun, has no sense of style and talks funny. I mean how did she even end up as the Charles Holden's ward? She's clearly out of her element. It's like some eighties sitcom. Who knows what kind of ghetto cooties we'll get from hanging out with her."

The other girls started laughing.

"We'll be nice to her until I get what I want and then we'll drop her," Nancy declared.

Tears streamed down Krystina's face unheeded. She should have known their friendship was too good to be true because the signs had been there all along. They were always asking about the people in her household, Uncle Charles in particular. Nancy was the most aggressive in her questioning. Now she got it.

Dominic pulled her away from the door. "Nice group of friends you have there," he taunted.

"I hate you," she whispered, shoving the bowl of popcorn and drinks in his hands before taking off downstairs. Krystina found refuge in the library and didn't come out for over an hour while she cried her eyes out. She couldn't face those girls in the state she was in. When she felt that she could at least look at them without crying, she finally returned to her room only to find them all gone. She wasn't sure what happened and frankly she didn't care. When she returned to school the following Monday, they all acted concerned for her well-being *and she called them on their bullshit which escalated to her slamming Nancy's head against a locker and mushing Emily in the face.*

Krystina hated herself for resorting to violence when none of those girls were really worth her time. But because she put her hands on two students, she was expelled and was shipped off to boarding school. Dominic had finally managed to get her out of the house at least temporarily, and all he had to do was once again, show her how unloved and unwanted she'd always be and for that, she knew she could never forgive him.

She felt her heart in her throat as she relived those memories when she was still so full of pain and anger that she wanted to lash out at the world. Dominic Holden always found a way to push her buttons. But now that she was all grown up, she refused to let him hurt her again. If he even tried to get beneath her skin, she'd come back at him at full force.

Once she was finished with her toilette, dressed in an off-the-shoulder pink top and cream pants and face adorned with light makeup, Krystina stared at herself in the mirror. She was ready to slay any demon, particularly the one waiting downstairs.

Taking a deep breath, she whispered, "I've got this."

Chapter Three

Dominic sensed Krystina's presence before he saw her approach the dining room table. Lowering his glass of merlot, he leaned back in his chair to observe her without obstruction. Gone was the gauche little girl who seemed so uncomfortable in her skin. In her place stood a woman with the regal bearing of a queen. Her confident strides ate the floor as she moved closer to the table. For a second, his breath caught in his throat as she drew near.

"Uncle Charles!" She focused her attention on the patriarch of the family sitting at the head of the table.

"Krystina, my child." The old man's face lit up and he held his arms out to the younger woman, accepting her into his embrace. "So glad you could join us for dinner this evening. You're looking well. Travel has been good to you. I'd like to hear all about your adventures."

Krystina chuckled, pulling away. "Weren't my letters enough? I don't want to bore everyone with my stories. I'd much rather hear how you've been doing."

"Letters aren't the same as an in-person account," Charles countered. "Besides, there were periods of times when we didn't hear from you. Of course, I was worried."

Krystina dropped a kiss on top of the old man's head. Well, I'm here now. And I don't plan on going anywhere at least for the next several weeks. That should give me more than enough time to regale you with all my escapades."

Dominic slowly took a sip of his wine as he watched Krystina move to an empty chair in between Felix and his grandfather. While she gave a Felix a friendly smile, it didn't escape Dominic's attention that she had completely ignored his presence. He almost expected it. But, she wouldn't be ignoring him much longer. He'd see to that.

He placed his glass down and fixed his gaze on Krystina, taking in every detail of her rich mahogany colored skin. "So now that you've done your stint of humanitarianism, what next?"

She narrowed her eyes as she turned them in his direction. "Why do you want to know? Can't wait to get me out of here? Don't worry, I won't stay longer than I have to." She cut her gaze away and before Dominic could give her a proper reply she started speaking again. "So, Felix? Where's Poppy? I thought you were both out of school for the summer."

"Poppy is out on a date with some guy she's been seeing for a while. I think she's going to dump the poor dude tonight."

Krystina raised a perfectly arched brow. "Really? Why do you think that?"

Felix waved his hand dismissively. "The longest she's ever kept a boyfriend was two months and this kid is nearing his expiration date."

"That's an odd way of putting it. Poppy is young, she's probably just having fun until the right man comes along."

"And what about you, Krystina?" Dominic interjected. "Are you just having fun or have you found the right one?"

Krystina firmed her lips into a tight line before she answered him without looking his way. "I just returned from overseas. What do you think?" The tone of her rhetorical question told him all he needed to know. Regardless of what her answer would have been, it didn't matter because he had plans for her, plans that had been in the making for the past few years.

Krystina Jackson had been a major irritant to Dominic from the second he lay eyes on her. When she was a child it was simply because he'd resented her unwanted intrusion into his family. He'd disliked her on sight, mainly for what she'd represented. But as she got older, she began to get under his skin for entirely different reasons. He didn't know how it had started, one second he was annoyed whenever their paths crossed and then the next, he found himself physically reacting to her presence.

The turning point had been her sweet sixteen birthday party. His grandfather had insisted Krystina have a party at the country club they belonged to and that all the family was to be in attendance. Dominic remembered drinking heavily that day.

Dominic grimaced as he watched the scene of loud obnoxious teenagers practically dry humping on the dance floor in a display they probably called dancing. Why the fuck did he have to be here anyway? There was plenty he could have been doing at the moment, like overseeing the renovations of the company's latest resort. If his grandfather hadn't explicitly demanded his presence, he would have found some other place to be. Krystina wasn't even family. Why his grandfather treated her as if she wasn't some little interloper was beyond him. He sure as hell wasn't in the mood to celebrate any occasion on her behalf. He hadn't attended a sweet sixteen party since he was a teenager himself and he felt out of place at an event where he didn't understand the slang and the girls seemed to be in a competition for who could wear the least clothing without getting arrested.

He was completely over this party after the fifth girl approached him to dance, each becoming more provocative with their invitation. One young lady had boldly placed her hand on his chest and licked her lips suggestively. Dominic politely declined and parked himself at the bar, away from the party revelers. Most of the attendees were the teenage children of business associates mainly because Krystina couldn't offer up more than a few friends to come to her party. The only surprise in that was that she had any friends at all. Her less than desirable personality traits were enough to scare anyone away.

Fortunately, his grandfather had taken heed to his advice and shipped her off to a boarding school after her last physical altercation in school. Sure those girls she'd brought home with her that one time were a bunch of backstabbers, but it had been no cause for Krystina to actually break someone's nose. At least with Krystina only coming home for summers and school holidays, her influence over Felix and Poppy were minimal.

He glanced at his watch with an impatience that was growing by the minute. This damn party had been going for at least an hour and the birthday girl hadn't even made an entrance. Typical Krystina to be inconsiderate of others.

As if some divine force had read his thoughts, the lights dimmed and a spotlight appeared on the stage. The band which had been playing some loud rock song earlier changed tempo. His grandfather appeared in front of the mike. "I'd like to thank everyone for attending tonight. Our birthday girl has always held a special place in my heart. I've watched her grow from a little girl to a beautiful young woman..."

Dominic tuned his grandfather out after that. Rolling his eyes, he turned toward the bar for a refill on his drink. This was stupid and as soon as he could, he intended to get out of here. After his glass was full, he turned around in mid-sip and *nearly spit out his drink. Grandfather had stepped aside and now standing front and center was Krystina or at least it looked like her. But it couldn't be, because the young lady in the center of the stage was absolutely breathtaking and Dominic couldn't tear his eyes away from the sight she presented.*

Unlike her scantily clad peers, Krystina had opted for a white strapless floor-length gown with silver accents. Her dark skin practically glowed. Her hair which she usually wore in braids was loose and flowing around her shoulders in a halo of curls and waves. Her jewelry was a simple pair of pearl eardrops and a silver bracelet circling her delicate wrist. She reminded him of royalty, so regal and ethereal...like a duchess.

He couldn't hear a word she said as she spoke. Were her lips always that full and tempting? Where did those dimples come from? It felt like he was seeing her for the first time. Even as she walked down to the main floor, his gaze followed her every movement.

On first appearance Krystina's dress seemed modest enough, but on further inspection, he couldn't help noticing how the bodice clung to her breasts and as she walked off the stage, he saw that her back was nearly bare. The dress dipped dangerously low, almost, to the crack of a high-seated ass. The only thing holding her dress was a silver strap. He shifted on the balls of his feet as he felt the front of his pants tighten. Fuck!

What was his grandfather thinking, letting her wear that to this party? And what was the matter with him? No matter how she looked this was still the same Krystina. Even though she looked nice on the outside for one night, it didn't change who she was on the inside.

With that in mind, he downed his drink in one angry gulp and slammed it down on the bar before heading out of the ballroom. He had to get away from this place. Away from her. When Dominic was on the road, he kept driving until he was miles away from the country club. He didn't bother going home that night or the next, in fact, he fled the country to his family's Caribbean resorts, not returning until Krystina returned to boarding school.

After that night, he's spent the next few years fighting his attraction to her, not only for the fact that she was underage but the enmity he felt in her presence. But ever since he'd lost control and kissed her, Dominic realized it was pointless to fight whatever demon drove his body to react whenever she was near. The hunger that made his mouth dry whenever he got a whiff of her sweet scent. The desire that made his cock stir whenever she sashayed by.

Krystina didn't know it yet, but he was going to have her. He would use her and keep using her until he worked this unnecessary ache from his system. A smile touched his lips as he thought of all the ways he intended to take her as her screams filled the air. That grin grew wider as he thought of how he'd finally be able to not think of Krystina again when he was done with her. He didn't necessarily feel guilty. Everyone owed the devil his due and as far as Dominic could tell, her debt was steadily growing. Besides, he was certain she felt the spark when they'd kissed. He didn't imagine the way she'd pressed her soft breasts against his chest or the little moan that had escaped her lips when their bodies parted. Yes, he was certainly going to enjoy every second of what he had in store for her.

"Isn't that right, Dominic?" Grandfather's voice broke him out of his thoughts.

"I beg your pardon, what were you saying?"

His grandfather smiled indulgently. "Krystina was telling me about the job she has lined up as a translator but there's not as much travel involved as she'd hoped.

You were telling me the other day that the interpreter you usually take with you overseas has retired. I was thinking it would be a better fit for Krystina to work for you instead. The pay would probably be better, and she'd get to travel quite often."

Charles might not have realized it, but he'd basically given Dominic a gift. This was perfect. What better way to get what he wanted than to have her work in close proximity to him.

He smirked as he watched her squirm in her seat trying to avoid looking in his direction. "I think that would be an excellent idea."

Krystina shot him a sharp glare before cutting her gaze back to his grandfather. "Uncle Charles that's so sweet of you to offer but I have something in the pipeline and I've already made the commitment to accept their offer."

The old man smiled indulgently. "Ah, but you said yourself that you haven't signed a formal contract yet and that they keep pushing back your start date. Doesn't sound like a promising start to me. Now, I really have no say in how the company is run anymore because I've handed the reigns over to Dominic and he does a damn fine job, by the way, but it would be nice to have another family member in the business. Felix and Poppy aren't interested in joining the company in any capacity so it sure would make and old man happy if you would at least consider it."

Dominic bit his tongue to hold back a retort denying any familial connection. Krystina was not family nor would he ever consider her in such a capacity but it did suit his current plans to have her working close to him. "Yes, I think that would be an excellent idea. As my grandfather stated, Steve, the translator I took with me on business trips is no longer with us. You speak five languages, don't you?"

Krystina pursed her lips before answering. "Yes," she replied tightly.

"That's two more than Steve. You should consider working *under* me. I mean with me."

Charles took Krystina's hand and patted the back of it. "I know you're all grown up and you have a life of your own, but please keep this offer in mind."

Krystina stole a glance in Dominic's direction before returning her gaze back to his grandfather. She had the appearance of a cornered mouse. "I...I...uh...sure. I'll think about it but I won't make any promises that I will work for Holden's."

"That's fine, my dear. Considering it is good enough for me."

Dominic smiled at her baring teeth, "Oh, I have a feeling she'll come around. I'm almost certain of it."

Her nostrils flared as she curled her upper lip into a sneer. She turned narrowed eyes his way. "You can't tell me... I mean, I can't guarantee you'll get the answer you're looking for. Like I said before, I made a commitment and I feel it's unprofessional to go back on my word."

"But you also said you haven't had a chance to sign the contract yet," Dominic pointed out. "I'm sure you have some concerns about working so closely with me but I promise, you'll enjoy it. I know I will."

While Felix and his grandfather may have been oblivious to his innuendo, it was apparent that Krystina wasn't because her lips parted in a silent gasp.

She pushed away from the table in a sudden movement. "Uh, excuse me. I forgot something upstairs.

I'll be back." As soon as she was out of her seat, she scurried out of the room as if she was being chased.

"She probably had to go to the bathroom," Felix said with a mouthful of food.

Dominic knew better. She was running away. That was fine. He would catch her and once he had her there would be no escape.

Chapter Four

Krystina wasn't sure what game Dominic was playing, but she wasn't having any of it. Since she'd known him, he'd let her know in every way, shape or form that he didn't want her around and had gone out of his way to make her feel unwelcome. It didn't matter that she'd been displaced from the only home she'd known or had lost friends she'd grown up with. It didn't even matter that her grandmother had died after a few short months of living in this house.

She was an outsider and that was all that seemed to matter to him. From her observation of Dominic, he was very straightforward to the point of abruptness at times except for the few people in his inner circle. The only people he seemed to actually act kindly toward were his grandfather siblings and a few friends. But one would think when it came to her, Dominic thought she was lower than pond scum, so what was with this sudden about face? Krystina neither liked nor trusted it. Dominic was up to something for sure and she refused to fall into any trap he had set for her.

Maybe he was trying to set her up in some way to discredit her in front of Uncle Charles. Dominic always seemed to resent the closeness Krystina shared with her guardian.

Tonight, there was something different about the way he looked at her however, and it made her uncomfortable. When he'd stared at her, Dominic's gaze had a lasciviousness about it that made her squirm and recall that kiss she'd buried deep in her psyche. After he'd humiliated her with that kiss, something inside of Krystina snapped. It had been the final straw for sticking around this house, but not because she'd hated it.

It was because she did. More than she'd initially admitted. For a long time, she thought something was wrong with her and couldn't exactly figure out what it was. Most of the girls in her school were always talking about kissing boys and who was the hottest. While Krystina thought a few of the guys were cute, she never got those tingly feelings her classmates spoke of. Even the few dates she'd gone on had ended in disaster because while the kisses had been mildly pleasant, she didn't really feel anything. It had briefly crossed her mind that she might be a lesbian but girls didn't do anything for her either. Krystina had resigned herself to the idea of being one of those rare people who simply wasn't interested in any type of physical relationship.

But then she met Tyler Shaw. He was one of the kids in attendance at her sweet sixteen party. She didn't know the majority of the people there. Most were the business associates of Uncle Charles along with their children. It was sort of embarrassing that so many strangers were in attendance because of her pathetic social life, but there was no way she could let her guardian down by refusing a party that seemed to mean more to him than to her.

Tyler was the nephew of one of Uncle Charles' oldest friends. He'd been one of the few people her age who was actually friendly toward her that night. Besides the five people she herself had invited, the other party attendees were there because their parents had dragged them there. Most of their parents were probably there to strike business deals with the man himself which is why Krystina wanted the party to end as soon as it had begun. Tyler, however, had asked her to dance for several numbers. They'd talked and laughed throughout the event. He actually made the party bearable.

They'd exchanged numbers afterward and often talked and texted mainly because Tyler lived in another state. But the summer before her senior year of high school, Tyler was in the area visiting his uncle and Krystina was home on break and after finally arranging their schedules, they were able to hang out.

"I can't believe you've never seen Citizen Kane. *It was voted the greatest movie of all time." Tyler shook his head as he popped the DVD into the player. The two of them had originally had plans to go to the park. Tyler was going to teach her how to ride a skateboard. Krystina had been fully prepared to break every bone in her body trying but Mother Nature had other plans that day. Torrential rains had changed their plans to catching a movie, but when neither could decide which one to see, Tyler had suggested watching something from his extensive DVD collection.*

He'd come to Krystina's place because they would be afforded more privacy since Felix and Poppy were on some kind of school enrichment trip and Dominic, of course, was busy working. Uncle Charles was visiting a sick friend in the hospital, and Ms. Lakes was recently let go much to Krystina's relief. So she had the whole house to herself.

"You act like that's such an uncommon thing. The movie is old as hell. Ask anyone else our age if they've seen this film and I guarantee you, most will say they haven't."

Tyler rolled his eyes. "That's the problem with this generation, no one appreciates the classics."

Krystina giggled. "You sound like an old man. Hurry up and start the movie. I want to see what all the hype is about."

"Prepare to be blown away." He plopped on the couch next to her.

Krystina, who had been huddled under a throw blanket, spread part of it over Tyler's legs as she snuggled closer to him. As the movie continued, she realized that she wasn't enjoying it so much because the movie was as great as Tyler had hyped it up to be, in truth, it was pretty boring, but she liked how it felt being close to him.

With a head of gold ringlets, bright blue eyes and a face full of freckles, he had the type of boyish good looks that would make any teenage girl swoon, but what she really liked about him was how nice he was. He didn't have a bad word to say about anyone and he always texted her some inspirational quote whenever she was feeling down. She considered him one of her closest friends.

As the movie progressed Tyler would rub her thigh which was bare because she wore a jean mini skirt. The skin on skin sent shivers racing up her spine. There were even a few times when he would casually brush the side of her breast with the back of his band. His movements emboldened her to do an exploration of her own. She ran her fingers through his blond curls and massaged the back of his neck. Finally, he turned to her. "You're not paying attention to the movie, are you?" His voice seemed strained and his eyes had darkened.

"It's really not my cup of tea."

"That's because you're not paying attention."

"How can I when you keep touching me?" she returned breathlessly.

"I didn't hear you complaining."

Krystina grinned. "Maybe because I liked it."

"I'd like to kiss you."

Krystina leaned forward until their faces nearly touched. "I'm not stopping you."

That seemed to be all the encouragement Tyler needed before he pressed his lips to hers. This was her first real kiss. It was a little awkward, a bit sloppy but otherwise, it was nice. As they kissed and caressed each other, Krystina somehow found herself on her back. She didn't realize what Tyler's intentions were until his hand was halfway up her thigh.

She stiffened. He must have noticed her hesitation because he halted. "We don't have to go further than you want to. I just want to make you feel good." He kissed her neck to emphasize his point.

This was all new territory for her but she believed that Tyler would stop when she asked him to. Besides, his hands on her body did feel kind of nice, the warmth she felt between her thighs had spread throughout her body. She wanted his touch. Moistening her lips with the tip of her tongue, Krystina nodded with silent consent.

"Just tell me when you don't want to do this anymore, okay?"

"Okay."

He smiled and covered her mouth with his again. Slowly, he eased his hand up her thigh until he reached the seam of her panties. To her surprise, he slid them down her legs before tossing them to the floor. Krystina's brain told her to end this before they took things too far, but her body was on fire. She finally understood that feeling the other girls from school were talking about and she didn't want it to end.

She gasped when he touched her labia.

Tyler raised his head to look her in the eyes. "You okay?"

"Yeah, your hands are cold, is all," she giggled nervously.

"I think, I can warm you up." He ran a digit along her slit before pushing it inside of her.

Krystina inhaled sharply at the intrusion. It wasn't exactly unpleasant but it felt foreign.

Tyler gently moved his finger back and forth, slowly at first until that heat she'd felt earlier returned. "Tyler," she moaned his name.

"Feel good?"

She arched her back and raised her pelvis. "Oh, yeah."

"What the fuck is going on in here?" A thunderous voice demanded.

Before Tyler could get off of her, Dominic appeared and grabbed him by the collar, dragging him off.

Krystina scrambled to her feet and frantically scanned the floor for her panties but she didn't see them. She turned an angry glare in Dominic's direction. Once again, he was the constant rain on her parade. "Take your hands off him!" she demanded.

"Hey, dude, we didn't mean any harm." Tyler looked like he wanted to shit his pants.

"Get out." Dominic spoke in a low threatening tone that left no doubt in anyone's mind that he was on the verge of exploding.

Tyler mouthed the word 'sorry' before grabbing his shoes and scrambling out of the room.

"You have no right to tell him to leave. He was my guest."

"Under my roof. If you want to act like a slut, then you take it somewhere else. You will not behave this way in this house."

Krystina's face burned with anger. She hated this man down to the depth of her soul. "This isn't your house jackass. It's Uncle Charles' and I doubt he'd appreciate you treating the nephew of his very close friend that way. Tyler and I were just kissing."

"If kissing includes his hands between your legs then sure. But let's get something straight here, little girl. My grandfather signed this house over to me last year. It's really none of your fucking business why he did it, but I just want to make it very clear that you're only here by his grace. So yes,

46

everything in this damn place belongs to me, and if you object to that, then it's too bad. I suggest you conduct yourself accordingly while you're here. Do I make myself clear?"

Instead of answering his question, she raised her chin defiantly. "I hate your guts."

"Hate me all you like but you will act like a civilized human being while you're here. That boy is no longer allowed over here because, obviously, you can't handle yourselves without adult supervision. Now, get the hell out of my sight."

"Fuck you!" screamed at him before racing out of the room with tears in her eyes. He didn't have to talk to her like she was a child. She was mortified about what Tyler must think of her. But the most petrifying part of that confrontation between her and Dominic wasn't that he had caught Tyler and her together. It was learning that the house she resided in was actually Dominic's. She didn't want to be beholden to him for anything. She couldn't wait to get out of here and never see him again.

Later that night when went back to the entertainment room in search of her errant panties. She couldn't find them. In fact, she never saw them again.

Even though Krystina had said she'd return, she couldn't go back downstairs and face them. She'd prepared herself for Dominic's hostility ever since her plane had landed on US soil. She could have handled a silent or stand-offish Dominic but this nice guy act of his was something she didn't expect. He was playing a game she hadn't been prepared for but she wouldn't let him win.

She simply needed to regroup and think of a way to gracefully decline this offer of a job he'd made on his grandfather's behalf. Sure, she did indeed know several languages. One of the upsides to attending one of the best boarding schools in the country was their language immersion program where students could take classes in one of the languages they taught. It was there Krystina learned of her ear for other languages and not only that, she enjoyed them. She'd practiced daily and spoke online with native speakers. During college, she'd taken a semester in Spain. She'd mastered Spanish, French, Mandarin and German. She was working on becoming fluent in Japanese as well. In her travels over the last few years, she'd gotten the chance to practice her languages, which was how she was able to get a job in NY as a corporate translator.

Basically, the job would entail her translating contracts and sometimes interpreting for her bosses when they were talking to foreign clients. It wasn't the most exciting job prospect but it was at least something that offered a livable salary. She wanted to get out of this house as soon as possible and live independently away from here. Away from Dominic. As tempting as working for Holden Resorts would be, she'd be dealing with the devil on a daily basis, and Krystina found a spit sandwich more appealing than working with that monster.

She paced her room, trying to exert the excess energy flowing through her when she heard a loud rap on her bedroom door. Figuring it was Felix checking on her, she opened her door without asking who it was. Big mistake.

Standing on the other side with a lopsided grin on his face was Dominic. "We need to talk."

"Go away." Krystina attempted to slam the door on him but he was too quick for her.

He pushed his way into the room and closed the door behind him.

"What the hell do you think you're doing? I don't want to talk to you right now. I haven't been back for a full 24 hours and already you're starting shit. Can't I just have one night back without having to put up with you?"

He raised a brow. "You're going to have to put up with me a lot more soon enough."

She narrowed her gaze. "What's that supposed to mean?"

"It means, you'll be working for me soon."

"Like I already said, I have another job lined up. If your Holden Resorts was the last company on Earth, I would rather go unemployed."

"You see, that's where you're wrong, Krystina, you will work for me."

"Are you deaf? There's nothing you could say that would make me work for you."

He chuckled as if she'd just told the funniest joke. "You see that's where you're wrong again because one, you don't want to disappoint your precious Uncle Charles and two, because I own you."

Chapter Five

Krystina opened her mouth to speak but the words were stuck in her throat. Dominic had said some outrageous things to her in the past but his last statement was beyond comprehension. And what was worse, he seemed to enjoy the fact that he'd made her speechless.

He smirked as he stalked toward her. "Cat got your tongue?"

As he moved toward her, she took several steps back. "Y-you...stay where you are!"

"Why? I thought we were having a friendly conversation."

The smugness oozing in his voice was enough to snap Krystina out of her stupor. Placing her balled fists on her hips, she glared at him. "Let's get something straight. I'm only here because Uncle Charles asked me to be. I'm fully aware that this is your house and I will be cognizant of that fact during my very short stay here. But my being here doesn't mean you get to dictate my comings and goings and it sure as hell doesn't mean you own me. In case you haven't gotten the memo, slavery ended years ago. I'd rather be dipped in honey and then covered in fire ants than work for you."

He slowly licked his lips with his tongue. "Mmm. The image of you dipped in honey has promise."

"You're being gross. Just get out!" Krystina attempted to show him to the door but he halted her progress by grabbing her arm.

"We're not finished."

She tried to yank her arm away but his grip was too strong. "As far as I'm concerned we are and if you don't let me go, I swear I'll scream."

"And then what? Who's going to come to your rescue? My grandfather? By the time he makes it up the stairs, I'll have all your clothes off with you beneath me. He'll think you were screaming in the throes of passion."

"There's no way I'd let you—"

He placed his finger over her lips. "Felix would probably make it upstairs quicker but again, I can make it look like we're two lovers caught up in the moment. Not that it matters because soon enough, duchess, I'll have you screaming…from pleasure."

By the time he finished speaking, Krystina was seething. She didn't understand what was going on. For years, she and Dominic couldn't stand the sight of each other and now he was acting as if they were in the middle of some sordid affair. "This isn't funny, Dominic. We hate each other. If you're acting this way to punish me for some reason, then cut it out. I'll stay out of your way and you stay out of mine and I'll be out of this house as soon as I find suitable accommodations."

A half-smile tilted his lips as mischief gleamed in his aqua stare. He stroked the inside of her wrist with the pad of his thumb. "But here's the thing, duchess, maybe I want you around. I wasn't playing a game when I said I owned you. From the moment I kissed you, you were mine. And you knew it too, that's why you ran away for three years. You felt it, too."

"Felt what? Whatever you imagine I felt is in your head, because as I recall, you forced yourself on me. That's why I left. I refused to live here after you assaulted me. But now, I realize that it was a mistake coming back."

Dominic chuckled. "Oh, no, duchess. I didn't imagine the way you moaned into my mouth or the way your nipples puckered against that thin top you wore. I also didn't make believe the heat emanating from your pussy. If either one of us is in denial, it's you, my dear. You might have thought that after all this time I would have forgotten, but I haven't. Now that you're back, I'm not going to let you get away so easily."

Krystina gasped at the boldness of his declaration and began her struggle anew to free herself from his grip. "You're disgusting."

With seemingly little effort, he yanked her against him and wrapped his arms around her, holding her prisoner. Before Krystina could open her mouth to protest, he covered her mouth with his. She couldn't believe this was happening again. This was Dominic! Her mortal enemy. The man who'd made her cry so many times, she'd lost count. She hated this man with every fiber of her being. Yet here she was in his arms and just like the first time he'd kissed her, she felt a warmth spread throughout her body. This wasn't supposed to happen again.

Krystina twisted her head, tearing her lips from his. Dominic grabbed a handful of her hair to hold her head steady while still holding her tightly with one sinewy arm. He was much too strong for her to break out of his hold. "Stop it. This is wrong," she attempted to appeal to any sense of decency he might have.

He raised a dark brow. "If that's the case, then why are you trembling?"

"Because I'm angry! I hate your guts," she spat.

"That so? How about we put it to the test?" He captured her lips again, cutting off anything else she would have said.

Krystina was determined not to respond but something unexpected happened. Instead of the aggressive kiss she'd been expecting, his lips were gentle against her. He peppered butterfly kisses across her mouth. He then ran his tongue along the seam, probing slightly.

As if her body had a mind of its own, an incredible heat began to build within her core and spread along every single nerve in her body. Unable to help herself, Krystina released a soft sigh. Taking advantage of her slightly parted lips, Dominic pushed his tongue inside her mouth, tasting and exploring her. Though he still held her head immobile, he'd relaxed his grip enough for Krystina to tilt her head, allowing him to deepen the kiss.

Her breasts grew heavy and the tingling sensation in her pussy made her squirm. Her knees grew wobbly and she didn't know how much longer her legs would be able to support her.

Dominic seemed to sense her thoughts because before she realized what was happening, he released the firm hold he had on her, scooped her up and carried her the short distance to the bed. Not giving Krystina a chance to react, he fell on top of her and returned his mouth to hers. This time the kiss wasn't as gentle as before. This one was hard, dominating and demanding. He sucked her tongue into his mouth and gave it a sharp nip, making her cry out.

He raised his head and buried his face against her neck with a groan. "You have no idea how long, I've wanted to do this," he muttered against her heated skin.

Krystina's mind was in a haze. She could barely think straight. She could only feel. Her nipples were now rock hard and she had to squeeze her thighs together to temper the fire Dominic had ignited.

He cupped one aching breast in his large palm and gave it a squeeze. Krystina arched her back to meet his touch. "So responsive, just like I knew you'd be." He slid down the length of her body and gripped the top of her pants. Slowly, he slid them down her hips, pulling her panties along with them.

If she was thinking coherently, Krystina would have kicked him in the head but some carnal demon had taken hold of her body and she wanted more of Dominic's kisses and caresses. With each inch of flesh he exposed to his hungry gaze, he pressed his lips against it, causing her to wiggle in delight. When she was naked from the waist down, he nudged her thighs apart and settled between them.

He licked his lips as if he were a starving man and he'd just stumbled upon a buffet. "You're so wet, your juices are running down the insides of your thighs." Dominic dipped his head and ran his tongue along her inner thigh.

"Oh, God!" she cried out.

He raised his head to meet her gaze. His eyes had darkened to the point where they almost appeared cobalt. "Not God, Dominic. And don't forget it," he growled before returning to his task. He ran a finger along her damp slit. "So slick and it's all for me." Gently, he parted her labia. "Mmm, such a pretty pussy, so pink and wet and ready for me. I'm going to taste you now,

Krystina. If you want me to stop, now is the time to say so because once I start I'm not going to quit until I'm finished eating your delectable looking cunt."

His words sent a shiver racing up her spine.

She couldn't talk even if she wanted to. All she could manage was a weak nod of her head. The rational part of her was telling Krystina that she'd regret this when it was over but her hormones were working overtime and she wanted—no, needed his mouth on her. She was on fire and only he could extinguish it in that moment.

Though she hated to admit it, the very first time Dominic had kissed her, she did feel something. Krystina thought at the time it was because of her lack of experience, but she'd since had a few lovers and none of them had come close to making her this damn hot. Sure, they had been pleasant experiences, but they weren't quite like this. Perhaps there was an added thrill to being intimate with someone she couldn't stand, but for whatever reason, the caress of Dominic's tongue against her skin was driving her absolutely insane with lust.

"Say it, Krystina. Tell me to stop."

The words were stuck in her throat and the only sound she could produce was a soft moan. A sinister smile curved Dominic's lips and at that moment, Krystina didn't know whether to be excited or scared.

After pushing her legs even farther apart, he parted her damp folds and bumped her clit with his nose. "Your scent is intoxicating. I bet it tastes as good as it smells." He caught her clit between his lips and sucked gently at first. Unable to keep still, Krystina writhed and wiggled until Dominic placed a hand on her stomach to hold her steady. He gave her clit a sharp nip, causing her to yelp more in shock than in pain. He then sucked on the bundle of nerves with the fervor of a man desperate to drive her to a mind-shattering climax.

As he kept her steady, Dominic, roughly shoved two fingers inside of her pussy. His lack of finesse surprised her more than anything because of the way her body soared in response to his savagery. As he eased the now slick digits in and out of her wet hole, he briefly lifted his head to catch her gaze. "You're so fucking tight. Imagine my cock inside this pretty little pussy."

The very thought of that image was nearly enough to send her to the edge of oblivion. Krystina moved her head from side to side as Dominic continued to fuck her with his fingers. He took her clit between his teeth this time and bit down. Hard.

She screamed, but he didn't let go. Instead, Dominic sucked the aching bud into his mouth again. He moved his fingers in and out of her with frenzied motions and then bore down on her clit once more, delivering the kind of pained pleasure that sent her soaring. Her orgasm was swift and powerful, rolling throughout the depths of her being. "Dominic!" she cried out before she realized what she'd actually said.

Removing his fingers, he lapped at her pussy, licking her juices with the broad side of his tongue. Sheer bliss flowed within Krystina and she couldn't hear, see or think straight. All she could do was feel the naughty things he was doing to her.

Just when she didn't think she could take another second of this delicious torture, Dominic raised his head. Without breaking eye contact, he put the fingers that had been inside of her, in his mouth and proceeded to suck and lick off her juices. "Mmm. You taste even better than I thought you would."

To her surprise, he rolled off the bed and adjusted his pants to reveal a rather large erection, but instead of taking his clothes off like she thought he would, Dominic simply stood there and watched her with an unreadable expression on his face.

Feeling exposed beneath his gaze, she closed her legs and sat up. How could she have allowed things to go so far? And, with this man to boot? Had it really been that long since she'd had sex that the first man to touch her in months could make her respond to him like some wanton sex-addict? She hated this man but hated herself more for giving in to her baser needs. She had no idea how she'd be able to stay here after this. She couldn't. The thought of disappointing Uncle Charles sucked. But how did she know that he wouldn't try something again, or that she wouldn't let him? That is what scared her the most. Finally, finding her voice, she whispered, "I...I think it's best if you left."

He nodded but not before moving closer to the bed. When he leaned over, she thought he would kiss her. Krystina flinched away but he simply moved his mouth closer to her ear. "This isn't over, duchess it was—"

She shook her head vehemently as she hugged her knees to her chest. "No. This can't, no won't happen again. It was an aberration and neither one of us was thinking clearly."

"I see. Now that you've had your say, let me have mine. You can convince yourself all you'd like that this is a one-time thing and that you weren't in your right mind to justify screaming my name while I ate your pussy. But, I'm not in the same denial. For the first time in a while, I'm thinking quite clear and this *will* happen again. A lot. And, you're going to love every second of it. It's like I said before, I own you."

He backed away, walked across the bedroom and out the door leaving Krystina trembling.

Chapter Six

Dominic could still taste her on his lips. And yet, the time he spent between her legs, feasting on her sweet pussy was not enough. It was all he could think of. Even as he sat through a meeting that could change the course of his company. He remembered her soft moans and the way she'd screamed his name. He could practically feel her nails grazing his skin.

If he wasn't careful, she could easily become an addiction and that wasn't what he wanted. He needed to stick to the plan so he could finally exorcise the demon that controlled him whenever she was near.

It had been a week since he'd confronted Krystina in her bedroom and everything was falling into place. The job she'd had lined up was no more. Krystina thought she could thwart him by taking that position she'd had lined up but he was certain she didn't count on the extent of his connections. After doing some research, he'd learned that she was set to work for a marketing firm that held several international accounts. It just so happened that this particular company had been in contact with his to set up a business relationship. Once Dominic had attained this bit of information, it was easy to get that firm to sever ties with Krystina. Of course, she didn't know why she'd gotten a call from their Human Resources department to inform her that they'd decided to go in different direction except that it had left her without a job.

Taking advantage of that fact, Dominic had hedged his bets by telling his grandfather that Krystina had decided to work for him after all before she had a chance to say no. Once that was accomplished, she could hardly say no to the old man who was clearly delighted.

A smile touched his lips as he remembered the fire in her eyes when she'd discovered what he'd done.

Looking through contracts was the least favorite part of his job, but he wanted to be thorough before sending them off to his lawyers. The expansion for the Holden Resort in Ibiza was one of his top priorities at the moment and he'd been pulling some pretty late hours to make sure everything was going according to plan, even bringing work home as he was doing now. His home office was in the back of the house away from the living quarters and when he was here, the rest of the residents in the home knew not to disturb him. So when the door crashed open, he didn't have to raise his head to see who the intruder was.

He felt her presence.

It took a considerable amount of will power to not smile, instead, he kept his gaze focused on the work before him, even though he couldn't see a word of it.

"You son of a bitch." Her words were spoken softly but there was no denying the anger behind them.

With slow, deliberate movements, he put his paperwork down, took off his reading glasses and set them aside and finally he raised his head to meet her angry gaze. "Krystina," he nodded in acknowledgment of her presence. "What can I do for you?"

She narrowed her already angry eyes. "Why the hell did you tell Uncle Charles that I'd agreed to work for you? I did no such thing."

Dominic leaned back in his chair and locked his hands together beneath his chin. "And here I thought I was doing you a favor, after all, you are out of a job."

"I'd rather shovel elephant dung than work for you! You knew by telling Uncle Charles that lie that it would be hard for me to dissuade him otherwise. I don't know why you have this sudden need to have me around because you sure as hell showed and told me in many ways that you hated me as much as I hate you."

He raised a brow. "Did I ever say I hated you?"

"You told me many times how I didn't belong here and that I was an interloper. You may not have said that you actually hate me, but you didn't need to. Your actions were enough. And guess what, I got the message loud and clear. So I ask again, what are you playing at?"

"Maybe I'm ready to bury the hatchet."

She rolled her eyes skyward. "The only place I'd like to bury a hatchet is in your skull. How the hell am I supposed to tell Uncle Charles that I'm not working for you?"

"You don't. You saw how happy he was when he found out. He considers you family and it pleases him that you'll be working for our company. Besides, I will be sure that your pay and benefits exceed what you would have been offered at the job that fell through. Plus, you like to travel and this job will involve a lot of it. In fact, we're going to Ibiza in three weeks and I'd like for you to come along with my team."

Krystina furrowed her brow. "Am I talking to myself? I said, I wouldn't work with or for you."

Dominic stared at her in silence amused at how flustered she was, knowing that by keeping quiet she'd get angrier and then he'd have her where he wanted her.

"Well?" She stamped her foot and crossed her arms.

"Well, what?"

"When are you going to tell him that I'm not working for you, because I sure as hell won't? It's your lie and it's up to you to fix it."

Dominic opened the lower drawer of his desk and pulled out a pair of scissors, some nylon rope, and a pair of handcuffs. He'd been preparing himself for this moment for a while but he didn't think it would happen this soon or this way, but he wasn't going to let this opportunity pass now that it was presented to him.

Once he placed the items on his desk in plain sight and closed his drawer, he stared at Krystina, waiting for her next move.

She took a step backward. "What is that for?"

"You know, duchess, when someone gives you an olive branch, the graceful thing to do would be to accept it, lest you want to be labeled a brat. And right now, you're being a brat. And do you know what happens to brats? They get punished."

Krystina's eyes widened to the size of saucers as she spied his tools. "What...what are those for?"

"I'm not a fan of repeating myself but I'll do it this one time. Brats get punished." He stood in one swift movement.

It was clear in that moment that Krystina realized Dominic wasn't joking. She turned on her heel and made her way to the door but he was faster. Catching her around the waist he pulled her against him, her back flush to his chest. She struggled in earnest and scratched his arms to break free from his grip. "Let me go, you bastard!"

Ignoring her words, Dominic managed to wrangle her to his desk. Krystina brought her foot down hard on his but unfortunately for her, she was only wearing a pair of soft ballet slippers. She caused more harm to herself than to him.

"Ouch, let me go, you big creep. Is this how you get off? Assaulting me?"

The more she fought, the harder Dominic's arousal grew. By the time he managed to bend her over his desk, he was rock hard. "It's funny how you mention 'getting off'. Oh, I intend to soon enough, but first, it's time for you to learn a very valuable lesson. Using the lower half of his body to keep her pinned to the desk he secured both her wrists in one hand and grabbed the handcuffs with his other.

She gasped. "What are you doing?"

Dominic didn't think that question deserved a response because it should have been pretty obvious what his intentions were. She attempted to buck him off by shoving her rear into his crotch. A groan slipped passed his lips from the contact of her ass hitting his erection. He nearly lost his grip on her but managed to hold firm. Gritting his teeth, he quickly snapped the cuffs on her wrists, locking them together.

"Let me go, Dominic. This isn't funny."

"Who's laughing?" He positioned her so that her upper body was stretched across his desk. There was a still hook on the side that he used to sometimes hang his jacket or other sundries but it was strong enough to use for the purpose he now had in mind. He slipped the chain of the handcuffs on the hook to hold her secure.

Krystina released a loud scream. "Dominic, whatever you're doing, stop this right now!"

He calmly walked across his office to the door and closed it. One of the reasons, he chose to have his space in this part of the house was because it was far enough away so that he wouldn't hear any of the noise from the other residents, not to mention, the room itself was soundproofed.

She could scream all she wanted because it was not likely anyone would come running because no one would hear, but he'd shut the door to show her the futility of raising her voice.

With a grin touching his lips, he walked back to the desk and placed a piece of rope on each of his shoulders. Dominic made a show of slowly placing the scissors back into the drawer. Then, he moved behind her. He was thankful she was *wearing a skirt. It would make it so much easier for what he had in mind.*

"I hate you so much and as soon as I get free, I will kill you."

He chuckled. "Don't make threats you're not prepared to carry through. Don't worry, duchess, when I get through with you, you'll be screaming for entirely different reasons." Moving behind her, he admired the way she wiggled her bottom in her attempt to get free. "You have no idea how sexy you look, bent over my desk like this. When I finally have you, I'm going to make it so good, duchess, but like I said before, this time around you need to be taught a lesson."

"The only lesson I've learned, so far, is that you're a prick, a sadistic prick."

Instead of replying verbally, he touched her bare legs and slowly ran his hands up her thighs until he reached her panties. He immediately yanked them down. Krystina stubbornly tried to plant her feet so that he couldn't take them off but he was stronger. He raised one leg and then the other and finally stuffed her panties into his back pocket. Like her, they belonged to him now. Dominic proceeded to undo the button and zipper of her skirt before pulling that off as well, leaving her naked from the waist down.

A smile curved his lips as he noticed her pussy lips gleaming with moisture. Krystina might claim she didn't like what was happening but her body said otherwise.

With that done, he yanked her legs apart and took one of the cut ropes and proceeded to tie her ankle to the leg of his desk. She kicked him with her other foot but he absorbed the blows as he went about his task. Once the one leg was secured to his desk, he moved to the other leg. After inspecting his handiwork with satisfaction, he stood behind her to admire her full, round ass. Krystina had a killer body and her rear was the type that made any red-blooded heterosexual man want to ride it.

He caressed one round cheek with the palm of his hand. *"So beautiful,"* he murmured.

"Don't," she whispered as she began to tremble.

"Don't what? Tell you the truth?"

"Whatever it is you're about to do. Please…I don't want this."

"Oh? That's funny because the last time you said that, you were screaming my name after I made you come." To emphasize his point, he slid his finger along her damp labia before shoving his middle finger inside of her and wiggling it around.

She gasped.

"Cat got your tongue?"

Without warning, he pulled his finger out and swatted her bare ass with a considerable amount of force, making it jiggle.

"Son of a bitch!" she yelled out.

He brought his hand down again, harder this time and three more times. She bucked against him and fought against her restraints all while cursing his name. *"When I get out of this, I swear, I will kill you!"*

The more Krystina fought, the harder he popped her bottom until she went completely still. Despite the dark hue of her skin, he could still see the blood flow on her bottom where his hand connected. He pulled back then and watched her tremble. He noted the single tear that slid down her cheek but more notable was the trail of moisture that dripped down her inner thigh.

"I don't want to hurt you, duchess, but you're going to have to learn that sometimes that smart mouth will get you in trouble." He rubbed the fleshy part of her bottom in circular motions to soothe her heated skin.

Krystina released a soft moan. She didn't need to say a word for him to know that he had her exactly where he wanted her. Seeing her stretched across his desk with her legs spread wide and her cunt on display made the blood rush straight to his cock. It had been his intention to issue a little light discipline while making her all hot and bothered but Dominic didn't count on being overwhelmed with the need to fuck that tight little pussy hard and fast until he finally obtained the satisfaction his body longed for. He could smell her arousal and it was more than he could handle. If he didn't get a taste, he'd go insane. Wanting to preserve the sight in front of him, he pulled his personal smartphone from his pocket and quickly snapped a picture.

Then, kneeling behind her, Dominic molded her cheeks, massaging the abused flesh. "You have a beautiful ass, duchess." He leaned forward and ran his tongue along the section where he'd spanked.

"Dominic, please," she whispered.

"Please what? Tell me what you want. Do you want me to play with your ass? Suck on your pussy? I want to hear the words."

"Don't make me." Her pained whisper gave away her internal struggle. If he actually had a conscience where this woman was concerned, he would have stopped and let her go. But he couldn't. Now that he'd set himself on this course, there was no going back. He had to have her and make her want him as much as he wanted her.

He slapped her ass again. "Say it."

"Dominic!" she cried out.

Smack. "Say it!"

"You bastard," Krystina whispered, wiggling her rear which only served to excite her more.

Smack. Smack. Smack. "I'm not going to ask you again. Now tell me what you want."

"I want your mouth on me." She spoke so low, that he barely heard her. Dominic knew Krystina well enough to know that this small capitulation was all he was getting out of her and that would have to do for now. Besides, he could no longer hold out.

Parting her slick labia, he dove face first and sucked on her distended clit. The fat little bud came alive in his mouth. Krystina's pussy tasted like heaven. As he licked and laved her wet womanhood, he popped her rear, alternating between cheeks. The stimulation of his mouth combined with the force of his hand must have been too much for Krystina to handle because her juices gushed into his mouth.

Dominic lapped her juices, not allowing a single drop to escape. His next instinct was to stand, free his cock and slide it home into her heat but he had to bide his time. If he pushed too far, he could lose sight of his ultimate goal.

With a great amount of willpower, he stood up and went to the washroom that was connected to his office. He closed the door so that Krystina couldn't see in and recognize how close he'd come to losing control. Dominic quickly unfastened his pants and freed his cock. Gripping it in his fist, he stroked himself, pumping it to relieve the ache that had built up in his balls. As he neared his release, he grabbed a tissue and shot his seed into it to avoid making a mess. Once his breathing was under control, he discarded the evidence of his desire, washed his face and hands in the sink and readjusted his clothing.

When he felt that he could handle being around Krystina again, he returned to his desk. Instead of releasing her, he took a seat at his desk and grabbed his contracts. Though he couldn't read a single word of what was in front of him, he pretended as if they had his full attention.

"Dominic...are you going to let me go?"

He raised his head. "No." It was all he said before returning to his contracts. Absently, he reached out and ran a hand along the curve of her ass, drawing a sigh from her sweet lips.

"Please. What if someone comes by and sees me like this?"

"Then I guess, they'll get a free show."

"Haven't you humiliated me enough? Just let me go."

"This is part of your punishment. You haven't fully learned the lesson."

"Okay, you win. What do you want me to say? I'll say it."

"I thought, I already made it clear. This is to let you know that I'm in charge. I get what I want and what I want is you. You belong to me. And until you admit it, I like you right where you are."

She fell silent. He was surprised that she didn't have a snappy retort. Dominic was almost a little disappointed that she didn't put up more of a fight, not that it mattered. Her silence wouldn't deter him.

For the next hour, he looked through his paperwork and worked on his computer while alternately stroking her bare flesh. Occasionally he'd run his finger along her pussy, teasing her entrance but not fully going inside of her. He enjoyed the sound of her sweet whimper during these brief caresses. Just when he didn't think she'd speak again, she whispered. "I belong to you."

Dominic perked up. "Could you repeat that?"

"You heard me," she said with the defiance he expected from her.

"Louder."

"I belong to you!" Krystina yelled the words.

Dominic chuckled as he stood up. "Damn right you do and don't forget it." He unhooked her cuffs from the chain allowing her to stand. Afterward, he untied her ankles and finally he produced the key to unlock her from the handcuffs.

Once she was free, she quickly grabbed her skirt and put it on before turning a glare in his direction. "Where are my panties?"

"You mean my panties? Don't worry about them." He didn't intend on giving them back either. The last time he'd taken her panties, Krystina had been sixteen years old and he'd caught her with some little punk she'd was fooling around with. At the time he felt ashamed of what he'd done, taking a teenage girl's panties. But this time, there was no shame. In fact, he loved seeing the fire in her eyes when she realized he intended to keep them.

The smile on his face didn't last long because her palm connected with his cheek. "Asshole! Don't think for a second that I meant what I said. The only reason I uttered those disgusting words was so you would let me go. I just want you to know that this changes nothing. Sure, you're able to turn me on but I still find you detestable. Don't ever touch me again. And another thing, I'd rather drink sewer water than work for you. It's not happening. It's unfortunate that I have to tell Uncle Charles otherwise, but he'll get over it."

There it was: that fire.

Dominic refused to rub the side of his face even though it stung like hell. Instead, he used it as a reminder that he was dealing with a wildcat and as such, he'd have to be careful of her claws.

"There seems to be a lot of things you'd rather do than work for me isn't there, duchess? I think my favorite was when you said you'd rather eat a spit sandwich. Such creative euphemisms, but it won't change the inevitable."

"I could think of a lot more, you scumbag."

"Are you finished?"

His response seemed to set her off. "Asshole." Krystina turned on her heel to leave but he caught her by the wrist.

"Let go!"

"Not until you listen. One, not only will I touch you again, you're going to love every second of it. Two, you start working for me next week. You have no other job to go to. Turns out, Lawson Corporation wants to stay in our good graces to get a contract they've been angling for."

Her mouth fell open. "You messed up my job offer?"

"Let's just say, I gave you a better opportunity."

"I'll find something else."

"You start working for me next Monday."

"You can't make me."

"I can't?" He released her wrist and extracted his phone out of his pocket. Dominic pulled up the lewd picture of her stretched over his desk with her legs spread open. "I wonder what my grandfather would say about this picture. Would he think the same of his precious ward?"

Some of the color drained from her dark face, giving her an ashen appearance. "You wouldn't."

"I'd rather you not test me on it."

"You must really hate me."

"On the contrary, duchess. I don't hate you at all. And therein, lies the problem."

She looked at him as if she wanted to kill him.

"You can leave now. See you bright and early on Monday."

She glared at him one last time before storming out of the room.

And now it was Monday and he couldn't wait to check in on his company's new translator.

Chapter Seven

So far, her first day at Holden's wasn't too bad, but then again, she had yet to run into Dominic. Uncle Charles had suggested that they ride in to work together, but Krystina wasn't having it. She made sure to get up extra early that morning even before Dominic and head out before anyone was up. Declining the use of the family's driver, she borrowed one of the older model sedans in the garage.

Once she had a nice nest egg saved up, buying her own vehicle was her priority. She wanted to establish her independence as soon as possible and if that meant grinning and bearing it for the next few months, she would. At least at this job, she'd be well compensated according to the paperwork that had been delivered to the house by courier. Dominic had certainly been thorough. The compensation package would have been hard to refuse by anyone's standards. But, it literally felt like she would be working for the devil.

When she'd arrived at the office, no one was there except the security guard so she hung out at the local coffee shop for about an hour to calm her nerves. By the time she returned to the office building, the place was abuzz with activity. Once she gave the guards her name, she was met by a tall redhead who introduced herself as Eileen, the head executive assistant. Eileen looked better suited to be a supermodel than working in an office setting. The other woman was friendly enough but was all business which was fine with Krystina.

Eileen gave Krystina a tour of the office and where all the important locations were like the cafeteria, the conference rooms, and the executive floor which was where she would be working. Dominic's office was almost its own little office unit in itself. Behind a set of double glass doors was a huge receptionist desk and behind it was a few offices to the side which belonged to the directors. There was also a row of cubicles that belonged to the personal assistants. When they walked further back, there was a huge set of oak double doors behind which was Dominic's office.

After being led out of what Eileen referred to as Grand Central Station, Krystina was then led down the hall to a small office with a large view of the city. She was surprised that she was given her own office. Eileen had then left her to set up her space as she saw fit and informed Krystina that someone would be by to set her computer up. Her main function would be to help translate contracts and work with Non-English-speaking clients at the behest of the executives. Her job description required that she travel quite a bit and most likely Dominic would be in tow. That's what bothered her the most. How could she work in close proximity to that monster? He'd practically blackmailed her into taking this job. She didn't think even he would stoop as low as to do something like that, but she shouldn't have been surprised. He'd always found ways to make her life miserable since she was a kid. Now, he'd found a whole new way to get under her skin.

Unfortunately this time, however, her body was a traitorous accomplice. It was easy to hate him or even ignore him, but now that he was her boss, that was impossible. She hated that he could arouse her to the point where she was unable to think straight. How had this happened? She'd literally left the country to get away from him after he'd kissed her that one time. Krystina had thought that things would be different when she returned home. Dominic would have moved on with his life and pretend as if that incident had never happened. At least, that's what Krystina had intended to do. In fact, she was willing to be cordial toward him, after all, some years had passed and they'd both matured a little, but Dominic was as deplorable as ever. She didn't understand this new plan of attack of his and why he was so relentless in sexually humiliating her.

Maybe the best solution would be going overseas again. She did love to travel and photography was her passion. She just didn't see herself going to dangerous locations to capture those world famous pictures people saw in magazines. Her sense of self-preservation was too strong for that. If she could find a way to be a photographer full-time, she would. But in the meantime, she had to be practical and she happened to be good at learning new languages so here she was for the time being.

She was so caught up in her thoughts that she didn't notice anyone enter her office. A stout bear-like man with a full beard and a pleasant smile stood in front of her desk. Krystina nearly jumped out of her skin in surprise.

"I'm sorry. I knocked and when you didn't answer, I poked my head in. You seemed to be deep in thought. Is this a good time for you? I'm Mark from IT, by the way."

Krystina stood with a smile and held out her hand. "Oh, I'm Krystina. Thanks for coming. I didn't expect anyone up so soon. I understand these things take time."

Mark gave her a firm handshake. "Not at all. Mr. Holden runs a pretty tight ship around here so that everything runs smoothly."

She barely managed not to roll her eyes at the sound of Dominic's name. Of course, he'd be as big of a control freak at his job as he was at home. "Well, guess it makes sense when the big bad boss cracks the whip."

"Oh, it's not that bad. Mr. Holden is tough but fair. Actually, this is one of the best companies, I've ever worked for. The benefits can't be beaten and a huge plus is that employees get amazing discounts to stay at Holden Resorts that we otherwise wouldn't be able to afford to stay at unless we were one of the top guys. I took my wife to the Vegas location for a vacation last year and let's just say if it weren't for my employee status, I would have had to put a second mortgage on my house just to spend one night there."

Krystina nodded. "I can imagine." Holden Resorts was a small chain with twenty locations worldwide, but they mainly catered to the mega wealthy. Krystina had been to a couple of the stateside locations when her Uncle Charles had taken the family there and the clientele consisted of celebrities, royalty and people with money to burn. Each location had helipads and airstrips because some guests preferred to arrive in their own private air crafts. The food was cooked by world-renowned chefs, the sheets on the bed were all made with Egyptian cotton. Every guest had access to their own personal concierge and a fitness trainer if they so choose. Every room was a suite that was equipped with a hot tub. At Holden's Resorts, the guest got to keep the terry cloth robes that were provided. The second a person walked into one of Holden's resorts, they were surrounded by luxury. To Krystina's knowledge, the cheapest room was thirty-five hundred a night. There were people who saved up just to dine in one of their restaurants.

"The people here aren't that bad to work with either. I think you'll fit right in."

She pasted a smile on her face. Mark seemed nice enough and aside from working closely with Dominic, she hoped everything else would run smoothly. As Mark began to set up her security codes on the computer, she asked him how he enjoyed his vacation, which steered them into a conversation about his family. He had a handful of amusing tales about his children that made her laugh. Somehow, she ended up teaching him a little French. Mark was horrible at pronouncing words. Krystina was actually enjoying her conversation when there was a tap on her door and in walked her biggest nightmare.

Mark was sitting behind her desk and Krystina was perched on her desk. She hopped off when Dominic moved closer. Being this close to him and a desk was too much for her nerves to handle.

"Mr. Holden," Mark smiled at their mutual boss. "I was just setting up Krystina's computer."

Dominic nodded. "Why don't you go ahead and finish what you're doing. I'll go ahead and take *Ms. Jackson* with me." She wasn't sure why he emphasized her last name the way he did, but the mood in the room changed from jovial to solemn very quickly.

He turned to walk out of the room and jerked his head forward, silently directing her to follow. With a heavy sigh, she followed him out of the room. She had a feeling that her day, that started out great, was about to turn shitty.

Dominic was annoyed to find that Krystina had left for the office without him. It was so like her to act childish about the whole situation. But what bothered him the most was walking into her office and seeing her smile and laughing with the IT guy. The rational part of his brain told him that it was completely innocent and the other man clearly wore a wedding ring. But when she'd turned her gaze in his direction, that smile had fallen. He shouldn't have cared that she wasn't happy to see him. It didn't matter how she felt, as long as he got what he wanted in the end.

He led her to his office and closed the door once they were both inside. Krystina stood by the door, even when he sat behind his desk.

"Have a seat, Krystina."

She shook her head vehemently. "Uh, that's okay. I'd rather stand here."

Dominic chuckled when he noticed her eyeing the door as if she couldn't wait to make her escape. "Thinking about the time in my home office? Don't worry. This desk is much too big for that...although there are a few interesting things we can do on it," he teased.

"You're disgusting. Did you bring me in here just to harass me? Because if that's the case, there are other things I could be doing with my time right now."

"In case you've forgotten my dear, I'm the boss, and what you do here is what I tell you to do. Have a seat. I won't bite...unless you want me too."

She crossed her arms across her chest and stubbornly stood her ground.

"Sit!" he roared.

She jumped before releasing a resigned sigh. Krystina sat in the chair in front of his desk and clenched her fists tightly in her lap. Not for the first time, he noticed how beautiful she was. Though professionally dressed in a pink blouse and a pair of fitted slacks, her clothing did nothing to hide her sexy figure. Her usually wild curls were pulled back into a severe bun that accentuated her high cheek bones. Dominic liked that she didn't cake her face with makeup. He hated that right now instead of making sure everything was running smoothly for her, he wanted to rip her clothes off, toss her on his desk and fuck her raw.

Dominic was thankful that the desk hid the hard-on that was now straining painfully against his pants. He took a deep breath before talking. "You must have gotten up early to get here before me. It would have made more sense if we were to ride in together."

"To be perfectly honest, the less time I spend around you the better. I may be working for you but I didn't say I'd commute with you as well."

"Still like making things more difficult than they have to be, don't you duchess?"

"Stop calling me that," she demanded through clenched teeth.

"Duchess? The name suits you, but you're right. I'll save it for another time, like the next time you're beneath me and screaming my name."

Krystina stood. "Okay, that's enough."

"Sit down, I'm not finished."

"Well, I'm finished with you."

"Not quite yet. I just wanted to let you know the itinerary for our trip at the end of the week."

Her eyes widened in apparent surprise. "What trip?"

"To Ibiza. I believe, I told you about it. I'm going to need your services. Our business partners speak perfect English but I'm sure you know there are plenty of times when a group may feel more comfortable speaking their own language when they're together. I need you to be my eyes and ears. I want you to help me make sure that the negotiations run smoothly. We'll be taking off on Thursday morning."

She didn't say anything at first and her breathing became ragged. Dominic didn't think she would respond but finally, she answered tightly. "And just how long will this trip be?"

He raised a brow. "What no argument?"

"Would it do me any good if I offered one?"

Dominic smiled. "Absolutely not. Glad you're finally seeing things my way and to answer your question, we'll be there for a week."

"I see. Well, if that's all that you wanted..." she stood up as if to leave.

"You know that's not all I want, but I was going to ask how your day was going so far."

"Like you care. Look, *Mr. Holden*, you may be my boss but let's get one thing straight. If you think anything is happening in this office, you have another think coming."

He was out of his chair in a flash and stood in front of her. "What happens here is whatever the hell I say happens. Now, you're dismissed."

Krystina slid out of her chair, but he was close enough that she had to touch him when she rose. She brushed past him and headed out the door. "I hate you." The words were muttered under her breath but he heard her crystal clear.

She slammed the door behind her.

"Hate me all you like, duchess, but it won't change the inevitable."

Chapter Eight

"Where are you sneaking off too? I've barely seen you these past few days."

With a sandwich and a bottled water in her hand, Krystina turned to see Poppy standing in the middle of the kitchen. It was true, she hadn't seen much of the younger woman since she'd been back. But that was mainly because most days, Poppy was out with friends and at night, she was out with her boyfriend, who apparently she hadn't dumped after all. Besides that, whenever Krystina was home, she stayed in her room or stayed away from the house by going to the gym or going to the park to take photos. She figured the fewer chances that she had to run into Dominic the better. It was bad enough that she had to work with him, but she absolutely hated being under the same roof as him, especially when she didn't know what to expect from him.

"Oh, I was just going to stream a movie on my laptop and call it an early night. When did you get in? I'm surprised you're not hanging out with your boyfriend tonight."

The blonde rolled her eyes. "Robert is getting too clingy. I mean, I really like him but he wants me to spend all my spare time with him. It's like he won't let me breathe. I told him, I had other plans tonight. Why don't you want to have dinner with the rest of the family? You know Grandpa likes us all to dine together when everyone is here."

"I know but work has been exhausting and I've been really busy packing and getting ready for my trip tomorrow. I've already talked to him about it. He understands."

"Oh, yeah, Dom was telling us about the upcoming trip. How do you like working for Holden's?"

Krystina shrugged. "I can't complain. It's not difficult work."

"There's a 'but' in there somewhere."

"No buts. I'm just adjusting."

"Is it because of Dominic?"

"Uh, what does he have to do with this?"

"I imagine, he's the reason you avoid everyone when you're home. You haven't been back very long and you've been making yourself scarce."

"How would you know, Poppy? You're barely here."

"No need to be defensive, Krystina. It's just an observation. If the problem isn't Dominic, is it me and Felix? Or just me? I mean, I know it's not Grandpa. He thinks the sun rises and sets on you."

If Poppy would have said that to her when they were younger, she might have taken that statement as jealousy but she knew that wasn't the case. When Krystina had arrived, not only did she have to deal with Dominic's outright hostility and an estate manager who made no secret that someone from her background didn't belong in a place like this; but she and Felix hadn't exactly been pleasant to be around either. Granted, they were children and they took the lead of their older brother. While Felix wasn't openly hostile, he didn't talk to her much. But Poppy's passive aggressiveness had been almost as tough to deal with as everything else.

Whenever the entire family would be together, Poppy would make sure to talk about something Krystina would not know anything about, basically excluding her. Whenever Krystina would walk into a room, Poppy would walk out. Things would go missing from Krystina's room and she'd find them in the strangest places, and whenever she did, Poppy would make an off-hand comment about the item to basically let Krystina know that she was the one who'd taken the object in the first place.

It wasn't until after Krystina had been shipped off to boarding school did things get better between her and Dominic's younger siblings. Felix was the more open of the two and she and him had actually become quite friendly. Poppy on the other hand, gradually came around.

Even today Krystina wouldn't exactly say they were very close but they were friendly enough and got along just fine, especially since the incident when Poppy was sixteen. Krystina had appreciated getting the occasional email from the younger girl during her travels.

"No, it isn't you or Felix. Why would you think that?"

A small smile curved the blonde's pink lips. "Well, maybe not my brother. But you have to admit, we haven't always seen eye to eye."

"Oh, if you mean that you used to give me a hard time, I'm over that."

Poppy sighed. "Krystina, I know I was just a kid then, but I never did apologize for being such a little jerk."

Krystina waved her hand dismissively. "Don't worry about it."

Poppy shook her head. "No. It's been bothering me a lot lately. Your last year of college, I felt that the two of us were finally becoming friends and I liked it a lot. You were like the sister I never got to know and when you were gone, I felt bad because I wish I wouldn't have allowed my own insecurities to get in the way of us becoming close."

While Krystina was touched by Poppy's confession, there was something in the way she phrased the part about the sister she never knew. She wasn't sure why she'd picked up on that part, because it was probably nothing but it just seemed odd. "Well, I appreciate it, Poppy, but that's the good thing about the past. We get to leave it there and start fresh. I know things couldn't be easy for you having a new person just show up out of the blue. It's my understanding that you'd lost your parents not too long before I came to live here and I understand loss."

"Yeah. I was going through a lot of things at the time, but it was no excuse for treating you the way I did. I was a little jealous, too."

This surprised Krystina. "Jealous of me? What for?"

"Grandpa paid a lot of attention to you. It made me question my place in this family, like I didn't really belong anymore."

"That's silly. You're his granddaughter. I was just his ward and you know how the saying goes, blood is thicker than water."

"But, that's the thing. Blood didn't matter. He's not..." Poppy paused and scrunched her face as if she wanted to continue her thought but decided against it. "Besides, you'd lost your parents too, I assumed. And, then your grandmother...she seemed really nice."

Krystina smiled at the thought of her grandmother. Willie Mae Jackson had been a tough woman, but she'd had a heart of gold. Krystina had been so lost without her and had it not been for Uncle Charles's love and understanding, she didn't know how she would have made it through those dark days shortly after her grandmother's passing.

"Thank you. I'm just glad that she got to live her last days in comfort. But please, don't beat yourself up about how you acted when you were a child. I wasn't exactly a pillar of society either. I was constantly getting into fights in school because I was always so angry and if it weren't for your grandfather's influence, I probably would have been expelled several times over. So let's not mention the past again, okay? Like I said before, this is a new day."

Poppy smiled revealing even white teeth. "Thank you. If I didn't get a chance to say it before, I'm glad you're back. I'm dying to hear about all the sights you saw on your world tour. But back to my original question, who are you avoiding?"

"Poppy…" Krystina spoke with warning in her tone.

"I'm just saying. I couldn't help noticing the way Dom was looking at you when he didn't think anyone noticed."

Krystina rolled her eyes. "I'd rather not talk about him."

"Fine. I just don't understand what it is about the two of you? Why don't you two get along?"

"Maybe because your brother is a dick." She groaned. "I'm sorry. I don't mean to put you in the middle."

Poppy laughed. "No worries. I know Dom can be a bit hard at times and I did notice that he didn't exactly give you an easy time when we were growing up. I just never understood why. I asked him about it once but he told me to mind my business."

"That sounds about right. Maybe when I get back from Ibiza, you and I can do something together."

"I'll be heading back to school in a couple days but we can definitely do something on the weekend. Maybe we can go on a shopping spree?"

"Well, my bank account is kind of slim right now, and I'd rather hold off making any big purchases until after I get a few paychecks saved up. Besides, I really need to get a car."

"You know Grandpa would give you his credit card if you asked, and we have accounts set up in a handful of stores. And, what's wrong with just using one of the cars in the garage?"

"I'm well aware, but you know I like paying my own way. Just because Uncle Charles has been extremely generous to me, doesn't mean I should continue to take advantage of it."

"But, he loves doing stuff like that for us. It makes him happy."

"And it makes me happy to have some form of independence."

"I bet you regret selling your car to help fund your world tour," Poppy pointed out.

"Not even a little bit. It would have been impractical to keep it while I was away and the money helped to support me as I lived out my dream." When Krystina had graduated high school, Uncle Charles had bought her a luxury SUV. Krystina had loved that vehicle but it had been easy to let it go when she had the option to travel.

"I admire that about you. Most people would be complacent and just let someone take care of them, but not you. I take it that you won't be living in this house for long. Grandpa mentioned that you'd planned on other living arrangements until they fell through."

Krystina nodded. "Yes. My potential roommate was someone I'd gone to college with. Everything was all set, but she decided she wanted to live with her fiancé instead. I understand, though. At least, this way I get to save up and the salary is nice enough for me to get a place on my own when I'm ready."

"Well, I hope you don't go too far away this time. I'm looking forward to us getting closer."

"Me, too."

"Are you sure you don't want to join the rest of us for dinner? I think Dominic is working late at the office. He probably won't be home until later according to Grandpa."

That thought perked her up. For the past week, she'd avoided riding into work with him, so she basically only saw him in the office. Knowing that he wouldn't be home made the decision easy for her. Besides, the cook always made something tasty and her sorry peanut butter and jelly sandwich couldn't compare. "Sure, why not?" She could at least have a relaxing dinner with people whose company she actually enjoyed.

Tomorrow, however, was another story. She'd have to tango with the devil.

Dominic took off his reading glasses and pinched the bridge of his nose to alleviate the pressure building up. The words on the computer seemed to swim together and he was starting to develop a hell of a headache. He wanted to make sure everything was in order before his trip in the morning. Usually, when he traveled, he'd take off early the day prior day to make sure he was all packed and sufficiently rested, but it seemed today was all about putting out fires.

First, one of the company's servers had gone down and he'd been unable to access some of his files. Next, he'd heard one of his contractors wanted to pull out because they didn't think the last contract negotiation had been fair. And on top of that, one of the security guards had been caught stealing boxes of supplies. Then, he'd nearly missed a key meeting with the board of directors and to top it all off, thoughts of Krystina crept into his mind throughout the day. The woman was driving him crazy and he hadn't seen her since yesterday.

He wouldn't wait to finally have her, so he could finally get her out of his system. The more she resisted him, the more he wanted her. Not for the first time, Dominic asked himself what the hell was the matter with him. This was Krystina! The perpetual thorn in his side since he'd set eyes on her. Out of all the women he had to be the most attracted to at the moment, why the hell did it have to be her? She was beautiful, no doubt. Yet he'd been with many beautiful women before, some of them pageant queens, and none of them had ever made him wake in the middle of the night drenched in a cold sweat with his dick rock hard with need. He'd observed her around the office for the past few days when she didn't think he was watching, and she seemed competent at her job. He noticed that she was friendly around other people, but whenever she turned that doe-like gaze in his direction, it was filled with nothing but animosity.

Dominic told himself that all he wanted from her was one thing, but he couldn't help but wonder what it would be like if she smiled at him. She had a great smile.

No! This wasn't how things were supposed to go. He didn't want to care about her and he wouldn't. He pulled a drawer open and took out a 6x4 picture in a silver frame. The blonde in the picture with aqua-colored eyes, like his, smiled back at him. Dominic wondered what she would have thought of what he was doing, and if she was proud of him.

He didn't get a chance to dwell on those thoughts because someone knocked on his door. Dominic quickly placed the photo back into the drawer and closed it. "Come in."

Jason Redmon, one of his closest childhood friends, walked into his office. Jason was his director of operations and was rarely in the office because he traveled even more than Dominic did. "Hey, man, I'm surprised to see your office light on from under the door. What are you still doing here? I thought you were going to Spain tomorrow." Jason walked further into the office and took the seat in front of Dominic's desk.

"You were here, so you already know what a disaster today was. I didn't get a chance to work on what I needed before I could go home."

"That's your problem, man, you have to be a part of every single dealing in the company. You don't have to be. That's the reason why you hire competent people to take care of these things."

"If I lose control of just one thing, everything else could possibly go to shit. I am in charge of thousands of employees and their livelihoods depend on my competence. It's my job to make sure everything runs smoothly."

"And, what the hell am I? Chopped liver?"

Dominic sighed. This was an argument that he'd had with his friend on many occasions. Would his life be easier if he handed some of his duties to others? Sure it would, but he knew that if he wanted to get a job done to his satisfaction, he'd have to handle a lot of things himself. It's not that he minded, in fact, it kept him busy and lately, it had been his sanctuary from indecent thoughts about Krystina. He couldn't stop thinking about her bent over his desk with her legs spread and her pussy glistening. He would have killed for a taste of her, right then and there.

"Earth to Dominic. Dude, where did you go just now?" Jason cut into his thoughts.

"Sorry, I guess I was daydreaming a bit."

Jason raised a brow in apparent surprise. "You? Is something the matter?"

"No. I just finished reading these emails. Any particular reason for the visit today?"

"Like I said, just stopping by when I saw your light. Hey, that new translator we have is fucking hot. When did she start?"

Something tightened within his chest and anger ripped through him. "That was Krystina." Dominic tried to inject as much calm in his voice as possible but he couldn't shake the sudden rage.

"The little ward your grandfather took in? Haven't seen her since she was a teenager. Since when did her ass get so fat? Goddamn, I never considered myself an ass man but shit, a guy can change his mind."

Dominic's fist clenched into a ball and he had the sudden urge to punch his friend in the face, instead, he said, "I'm sure Antonia wouldn't appreciate this line of conversation." Antonia was Jason's longtime girlfriend since college. It was a wonder she was still with Jason after all this time without a proposal. Most women would be hinting at a ring long before thirteen years. The woman apparently had the patience of a saint.

Jason waved his hand dismissively. "Toni understands how we men talk. She's not that uptight about stuff like that. Besides, there's nothing wrong with window shopping. So, when did Krystina get so hot?"

Jason was his friend, but at the moment he was really pissing Dominic off. "You do remember this is the same woman who called you an 'asshead'." Jason had come over for a visit while he was on college break and had stayed with Dominic's family for a few days. Krystina had pretty much stayed out of their way for the most part but once Dominic and Jason had walked into the family room to catch a football game only to see the brat watching some inane show. Angry to see the interloper intruding on his space, he'd snatched the remote control from her and told her to leave the room. Krystina, of course, didn't go quietly. She called them both a couple of assheads before storming out of the room. In retrospect, he could have been more diplomatic in the way he'd handled that situation, but at the time, he wasn't prepared to play nice.

Jason tossed his head back and let out a boisterous laughed. "Come on, you have to admit that was pretty funny. Besides, we did kick the kid out of the room when she was in the middle of watching a movie on television. I bet if it had been you, you would have been pretty pissed as well. I don't even understand why you gave her such a hard time anyway. It's not her fault that—"

"Don't say it."

Jason sighed. "Look, I'm just saying that I never understood why you took all your anger out on a kid. A kid who couldn't control the actions of the adults you should have placed the blame with."

Dominic briefly firmed his lips into a tight line. "I'm not having this discussion with you."

Jason shrugged. "Well, since she's working here now, I guess that means the hatchet is buried, then?"

"She works here now. Let's leave it at that."

"Fine. Don't talk about it. I just wanted to stop in and say hello. Hope your trip goes well. Maybe we can do dinner when you return?" He stood up to leave.

Dominic could only nod in response.

Once his friend was gone, he sat back in his chair and exhaled. He was probably a bit more curt with Jason than he'd intended to be, but the other man knew what a sore subject his past was. Besides his grandfather, Jason was one of the few people who knew the truth about Dominic's parents and why he'd resented Krystina's intrusion into his life. Perhaps what he had planned was wrong, but he didn't care. He couldn't care. Once and for all, he would exorcise that woman from his system, then he could finally close that chapter of his life for good.

The upcoming trip was certainly going to be interesting. Thinking about it, Dominic smiled for the first time that day.

Chapter Nine

Krystina didn't get a wink of sleep the night before, because the second her head had hit the pillow, she couldn't stop thinking about what Dominic might have in store for her. Twice, she'd allowed her baser instincts to take over in the face of his domination and she didn't think she could trust herself around him when he tried something again and she was absolutely certain he would. Despite her lack of sleep the night before, there was no way she was going to go to sleep now.

When she'd seen her itinerary, she saw that she'd be flying commercial which gave her some measure of relief because she knew that Holden's had a private jet. She thought Dominic would take that mode of transportation but no, Dominic was seated right next to her in first class. He'd said something about the jet being repaired and it would be ready for travel on their way home. At least on the private plane, she could put some distance in between them, but she couldn't when their seats were next to each other. She had the window seat which would have made it easier for her to take a quick nap if she wanted, but she couldn't trust that he wouldn't touch her in some way once she was unconscious. This eight-hour flight was going to be torture.

For now, he was working on his laptop. She stole a peek at him from the corner of her eye. He was wearing his horn-rimmed glasses and coupled with his prematurely graying temples he looked quite distinguished. There was never any question about his attractiveness but she hated that such a handsome face was connected with such a jackass of a man.

Without warning, Dominic took his glasses off, closed his laptop and turned in Krystina's direction.

"What?"

She flinched. "What are you talking about?"

"You've been staring at me for the past ten minutes? Obviously, you want something, so what can I help you with?"

She laughed nervously. "I wasn't staring at you. I was just staring into space."

"Your eyes were practically burning a hole in me. You don't fool me, duchess."

She snorted. "In your dreams."

He smirked. "You have no idea what I dream of and if you did, you'd probably blush."

Krystina turned in her seat. "Must you always be so nasty?"

"I'm just stating facts. I'm surprised you're not fast asleep. We have at least another six hours before we land."

"I...I'm not tired."

"You've always been a terrible liar, Krystina. Why don't you catch some shut-eye? Judging from those bags under your eyes, you could use some."

"Gee thanks. Aren't you the gentleman?"

"You know me well enough to have figured out that I don't beat around the bush. Fine if you don't want to sleep, then let's talk."

"Talk?" In the twelve years, she'd known him, Krystina could count the number of civil conversations they'd had with each other on one hand.

"Yes, talk. You know, when one person opens their mouth and words come out and the other person—"

"I get it, Dominic. No need to be a jackass about it. It's just that you and I don't really converse that much. We always end up fighting."

"Well, maybe I'm tired of fighting. And since I don't usually sleep on plans, a friendly conversation will help pass the time."

She sighed in resignation. What harm could it do? She'd be stuck with him for the next seven days, it wouldn't help either one of them if they continued to antagonize each other.

"So what do you expect we'll be dealing with when we get there?"

"If we're talking strictly business, you probably should have read your itinerary."

Krystina huffed in frustration. She knew this was a big mistake "If you're going to be a wiseass, let's just go ahead and terminate this conversation."

He sighed raking his fingers through his dark hair. "My apologies, I'm just a little on edge. I've had a lot on my mind."

"Wow, what day is this so I can mark it down? Dominic Holden is actually apologizing to me? The world must be coming to an end."

"Now, who's being the wiseass?"

"You're right. I'm sorry. This is my first official grown up job and I'm excited and nervous about it."

"Don't worry, I'm sure you'll be fine. Like I said, our business partners speak perfect English but it sometimes helps to have a translator around to hedge our bets. Sometimes when we're working with people from different countries, they may break off into a group and have a discussion in their native tongue. That's where someone like you would be handy to make sure everything is on the up and up. I'm not anticipating anything will go awry with the Sandoval group but one can never be too careful."

"So I'll basically be serving as your spy/assistant?"

"You got it." He paused for a moment before speaking again. "Now that we've got that out of the way, I'd rather not talk business. We'll have plenty of time for that in the next several days."

"What do you want to talk about?"

"Well, you were away for three years. Grandfather told me a little bit about where you were going and the countries you visited but I'd like for you to tell me about it."

"I'm not sure what you want to know. I mean, you're already aware that I finished my last year of college in Bristol. I loved the English countryside. When I wasn't in school, I explored the town and saw the sites. My favorite places to visit were the old manors that were open to the public. It was fascinating to see so many artifacts and things that you only read about in books. When school was closed for long holidays, I'd take a train to London and then another to Paris. I fell in love with that city from the food to the sights and sounds. The first time I stepped foot there, I knew I wanted to live there."

"But after you graduated, you hopped around the world. Why did you do that instead of settling in Paris like you wanted to?"

"Well, I did stay in Paris for a few months at the end of my stint overseas and maybe one day, I'll go back. But when I received that settlement, I realized I could do the practical thing and put it toward a house and my future or I could live out my dream and see the world. I know it sounds irresponsible but I feel like I did the right thing. I got to do some volunteer work and met some amazing people and formed life-long friendships. I experienced different cultures and witnessed wonders that I could only dream of."

Shortly after she'd received her degree, Krystina knew she wasn't ready to return to the US. She'd gotten a job at a coffee shop while she worked on a plan to stay for at least a year. Then, she'd gotten news from the states that she was the recipient of a trust fund that had been set up by her grandmother. Apparently, Krystina's mother, who'd struggled with addiction for years, had been admitted to the hospital after being assaulted by a dealer to whom she owed her money. Because of her history with drugs, the doctors apparently hadn't taken her seriously when she said she was in a lot of pain. They didn't bother to do any x-rays. To them, she was just another addict looking for a fix. She'd died from internal bleeding. Krystina's grandmother had told her that story shortly before she died. What she didn't tell Krystina was that the hospital had settled a large sum of money on her grandmother who set up a trust for Krystina which she was to receive upon her graduation from college.

That money had been more than enough for her to live on for a few years, if she budgeted wisely, and picked up odd jobs here and there. She didn't have a single regret.

"What was your favorite experience and country?"

"I enjoyed all of them but, of course, like I said France was my favorite. The city of Paris, in particular. But my most memorable trip was when I got to volunteer at an orphanage in South Africa. The children were so beautiful and full of light. They somehow managed to smile despite their circumstances."

Dominic didn't respond and when she turned to look at him, he was staring at her. She couldn't read his expression but there was something in his eyes that she hadn't seen before and it made her a little hot under the collar.

"Uh, Dominic?"

"Sorry, I was just thinking. Uh, I was surprised when you decided to stay overseas after you graduated. What gave you your thirst for travel?"

"My time at the boarding school, actually. There was a teacher, who I'd really connected with, who told me about his travels and I was fascinated. I wanted to see and experience everything he talked about. I was just a girl from a little town in Mississippi who didn't have a vast worldview. I mean before I went to live with you guys, I'd never even left my town. I think realizing there was a vast world out there waiting for me to explore, set a spark off inside of me. It changed me."

Without warning, Dominic leaned forward and placed his lips against her. Caught off guard, she didn't get a chance to protest and by the time she did, Krystina found herself melting against him. Before she realized what she was doing, she threaded her fingers through his hair. She could taste the brandy he'd drunk earlier mixed with a hint of mint. His lips were soft and surprisingly full. One thing was certain, Dominic was an excellent kisser and he made her body tingle all over.

He cupped her face in his palms, deepening the kiss as he pressed his tongue past her slightly parted lips. She pressed her tongue to meet his, licking him and swirling around his. Her nipples pebbled painfully against her blouse as she pressed her body even closer to his. She was so caught up in the moment that she didn't hear the flight attendant clearing her throat.

She pulled away from him like a teenager caught making out in the backseat of a car.

The brunette smiled at them with a hint of smug condescension. "I was coming to see if you two were interested in dinner."

"Uh, I'd just like a bottle of water, please. Please excuse me, I have to run to the restroom." She unbuckled her belt and slid past Dominic and the flight attendant. Once she was behind the lavatory door, she plopped on the toilet and rested her head in her hands. They hadn't even made it to their destination and already they were making out, how the hell was she supposed to make it through this trip unscathed?

Dominic wasn't sure what had come over him. One minute he was listening to Krystina talk about the last three years of her life and the next he was kissing her. He hadn't meant to because this wasn't the way he wanted things to play out. The last thing he wanted was to lose control of the situation, but the way her eyes lit up when she talked about traveling and the passion in her voice made him throw caution to the wind.

Listening to her, made him reassess some of the things he'd thought about her. When they'd first met, he was determined not to like her because he didn't want her around as a reminder of everything that he'd lost, and what he'd held dear. Whenever he saw her walking around his house as if she had a right to be there, his rage would boil out of control. Maybe he was crazy for taking an instant dislike to a child, but he couldn't help it. The pain of what he'd gone through was still too fresh to him. He'd just been starting to adjust to his new life and then *she* showed up.

To some extent, he'd resented Miss Willie Mae's presence, as well, but he knew better than to not show respect to his elders. So it was Krystina who bore the brunt of his hate. It didn't help matters that she was this angry little hell cat who got into fights in school and seemed angry all the time. He realized that she probably acted out because she had suffered losses in her life as well, but he didn't care. She looked too much like...

Dominic shook his head. He wouldn't utter that name, or even think about it. Maybe she had matured and wasn't the bratty child she used to be, but even still, it didn't change anything. He just had to remember his plan and stick to it.

He glanced at his watch for the third time. She'd been gone for almost a half hour and he was beginning to wonder if something was the matter. Did the kiss shake her up as much as it did him? Every time he touched her, tasted her, he craved more. Needed it. Soon, he'd have her right where he wanted her.

When Krystina finally returned to her seat, she appeared to be fine.

"You were in there for a while."

"Uh, yeah, I was having some stomach trouble."

"You're a horrible liar, duchess." He picked up the bottle of water the flight attendant had left and handed it to her.

She took the water from his grip with shaking hands "What makes you think I'm lying?"

"Your voice raises an octave and it shakes when you're not telling the truth. You know, you can't keep running from me."

She sighed. "Must we do this? I mean really, this is a business trip and I'd rather keep things on a professional level."

"And we will, but we'll also have a lot of downtime."

"Which I intend to use exploring the city. I've never visited this part of Spain before."

"Sounds like a plan. I look forward to it."

"You're not invited, Dominic."

He leaned back in his seat with a grin. "We'll see."

Krystina released an exasperated huff and turned away from him to look out the window.

She probably didn't argue because she knew it was futile. His plan would soon come to fruition.

Chapter Ten

Krystina was blown away by the beauty of the city. It was a beach town full of hotels, resorts, the ocean and beautiful people. She couldn't wait to explore it and take pictures. When they arrived at the resort, Krystina was blown away by the beauty of her surroundings. She'd been a guest at one of the Holden's resorts when Uncle Charles had taken the family to one in the US, but it couldn't compare to the majesty of this structure with its glass cathedral ceiling, marble floors and sculptures that looked like they were made especially for this location.

As they walked through the lobby, the corridor turned into a greenhouse filled with exotic flowers and colorful birds flying around as if they were in the middle of a rain forest. Seeing the majesty of this resort, it was understandable why a stay here was so expensive. From the second they arrived, Dominic was treated like royalty and so was she, by default. But that was the beauty of staying at a place like this. Everyone was treated as if they were VIPs. Javier, their own personal concierge, escorted them to their suite which was almost as big as the bottom floor of the mansion they lived in. The walls were gilded in gold and everything screamed money. Thankfully, it had two bedrooms even though Krystina would have preferred to have a suite of her own.

"If you need anything, please do not hesitate to call me." Javier smiled before Dominic nodded in dismissal.

Krystina headed to her room but Dominic called out to her. "You don't have to run off. I won't bite...unless you want me to."

"Dominic, not now. I've barely had a wink of sleep and I'm dead tired. I'd like to take a shower and then rest."

"You do that. I have some phone calls to make. We'll have dinner later tonight."

"What if I don't want to have dinner with you?" she challenged.

His face hardened for a brief second. "We'll have dinner later. Be ready." He then walked to his own room leaving her standing in the middle of the suite.

"Asshole," she mumbled and headed to her own room which was just as luxurious as the rest of the place. The comforter looked so soft and inviting. Krystina laid down for a minute with the intention of resting her eyes but found herself drifting off.

When she opened her eyes again, it was nearly dark outside. She pulled her cell phone out of her pocket and saw that she'd slept for three hours! She wasn't sure what dinner time was but in Spain, it was usually late. After taking a quick shower, she felt refreshed. As she was getting dressed, her cell phone rang. Krystina frowned. She wasn't expecting a call.

When she picked up the phone and saw who was calling, she smiled. "Uncle Charles! I'm surprised to hear from you."

"I wanted to check on you, my dear. The last time you went overseas, you didn't come back for three years."

Krystina giggled. "Oh, come on. You know, I'll be back in a week."

"I'm going to hold you to that. How was your flight? Did it go smoothly?"

"Yes. No hiccups."

"And that grandson of mine, has he been behaving himself?"

"Dominic has been Dominic."

The old man chuckled on the other end of the line. "That sounds about right. I never got the chance to say it, but I'm so happy that you're working at Holden's. This is the way things were meant to be. Now that you and Dominic are working together, the two of you will get along better."

It surprised Krystina to hear Uncle Charles say this because, despite their mutual animosity, she and Dominic tried not to argue in front of the older man so as not to upset him. "I don't know what you're talking about. We get along just fine."

"Krystina, my dear, you don't have to lie to me. I know how my grandson has been and I wish I would have spoken up about it sooner when you were younger, but I always thought everything would eventually work out. And when it didn't, that's when I agreed to have you sent to that boarding school but more for your own sake than anything else. And I dare say, I made the right choice. You seemed happier whenever I saw you."

He was right. Though a lot of the girls at the school were snobs, she did manage to make some friends and because of the excellent curriculum, she was able to thrive. "I was, but I'm sorry that you were so worried about me."

"Why wouldn't I be? You might not be my blood, but you've always been like one of my own."

Tears sprang to her eyes. She loved this man like the father she never knew. Despite everything that had happened to her from losing her mother, her home and then her grandmother, this man had remained a constant force in her life. Krystina didn't realize how much she'd needed to hear those words right now, especially when she didn't know what was going on between her and Dominic. It was one thing when they simply hated each other, but it was quite another when hormones were involved. Not only was she scared of giving herself to him, she feared that she wouldn't get out the situation unscathed. Knowing she had someone in her corner no matter what, made her feel better.

"Thank you. You have no idea how much that means to me."

"It's the truth. Your grandmother was very special to me, as was your mother. Their deaths were very hard on me and I made a promise to Willie Mae to make sure you were taken care of, but you're not just an obligation to me."

"I appreciate you saying this, but where is this all coming from?"

"I've just been doing a lot of self-reflecting lately. It happens when you're old."

"You're not that old. You still have plenty of life left in you."

Uncle Charles chuckled. "You're right. I'm not ready to tangle with death quite yet. Well, I don't want to hold you up. I know it's close to dinner time around there so I won't keep you. Just calling to tell you I'm thinking about you. Love you, kiddo."

"I love you, too. Thanks for calling." She hung up feeling better than she had in the past week.

Krystina dressed in a black spaghetti strap maxi dress. She piled her hair on top of her head and put on some eyeliner and lip gloss. It was way too hot to wear too much makeup. When she left her room, Dominic was standing in the middle of the room in a pair of khaki pants and black shirt. The top two buttons were undone to reveal tufts of dark hair. She gulped at the sight he made. Why did he have to be so sexy and why did she react to him the way she did? He was so detestable, yet she couldn't stop thinking about his hands roaming her body. Back home she could avoid him and come and go as she pleased, but here on this work trip, she was at his mercy. She prayed she could get through the next seven days unscathed.

His eyes seemed to darken when he took in her attire. "You look beautiful, duchess."

Unused to compliments from him, she raised a brow. "Are you being sarcastic?"

"You're a beautiful woman, Krystina. It's only natural that I'd take note of that."

"Well, uh, it's not like you've exactly had a lot of nice things to say to me over the years."

"Maybe, I'm trying to rectify that."

"Dominic, whatever you're playing at, can't we just get through this week without being at each other's throats. I don't need the stress."

He shrugged. "Who's playing? Just take what I said at face value and move on."

She ran the tip of her tongue over her lips in a nervous gesture. "Fine. Thank you."

"We'll be meeting some team members from the Sandoval Group at dinner. I thought it would be a good idea to have our first meeting in a more casual setting."

"So, this will be a business dinner?"

"Sort of. It's more of a getting-to-know-you situation. We'll first be meeting them at the bar for drinks and then we'll dine. Shall we?"

Krystina nodded, slightly relieved that there would be other people around at dinner to serve as a buffer between her and Dominic.

She allowed him to lead her out the door. He placed his hand on the small of her back which sent a shiver up her spine. She had a feeling this was going to be a long night.

Dominic tightened his hands around his glass of cognac as the tension within him built. This wasn't the way he'd envisioned his dinner going. It had been his intention to use tonight as the beginning of an aggressive campaign to get Krystina where he wanted her. In his bed. But so far, he had to sit back and watch Tomas Sandoval, the head of the Sandoval group, flirt shamelessly with her. And from the looks of it, Krystina didn't seem to mind.

Tomas was the president and CEO of one of the largest private tourism companies in Europe and a shrewd businessman which was why Dominic believed a partnership between Holden's and Sandoval would be a lucrative endeavor for both groups. Dominic had no intention of letting the other man's flirtation get into the way of their business dealing, but his patience was wearing thin with Krystina, who seemed to be eating all the attention up. When they began to speak in fluent Spanish with each other, Dominic nearly lost his cool.

Tomas turned to Dominic with a wide smile on his face. "Where did you find this jewel? She has beauty and brains. If you're not careful, I may have to snatch her away from you."

Krystina giggled. "Be careful about what you put out in the universe because I just might take you up on your offer."

Dominic finally reached his breaking point. "Well, I've known Krystina since she was a child. She's actually one of my grandfather's charity cases."

The smile that she'd been wearing fell and her beautiful mahogany skin took on an ashen hue. Dominic wasn't sure what had made him say something like that but he hated seeing her smile at another man in his presence especially when she'd never smiled at him like that.

The jovial tone at the table took a dramatic turn. Even Tomas shifted in his seat uncomfortably. The other two associates dining with them shot Krystina pitying looks before paying attention to their drinks.

Dominic swallowed the rest of his drink in one gulp never taking his gaze off of Krystina. She kept her head down and locked her hands together in her lap.

Tomas cleared his throat before breaking the awkward silence. "That sounds like a fascinating story, *cara*. I'd like to hear about it sometime? Perhaps over dinner, sometime this week?

Dominic flared his nostrils. "Krystina won't have time for that. Our schedules are pretty tight this week."

Tomas raised a brow but pressed the issue further. "Well, maybe another time. I trust the next time you visit this little island, I can give you my own personal tour. Or better yet, I could show you around our headquarters in Madrid."

Krystina could only nod. "That would be nice." Her voice was wobbly and if he didn't know better, he thought she might cry. But he must be mistaken. Krystina was tough as nails.

After a few more minutes of strained conversation, she stood up. "My apologies, gentlemen. I'm not feeling well and I'm going to have to excuse myself for the night. I look forward to seeing you all in the morning."

Tomas stood with her. "Would you like me to escort you to your room?"

"Oh, no, please. I'm fine getting there on my own. But thank you for offering and thank you for being such a gentleman."

Dominic felt that that last statement was somehow a shot at him. Perhaps, he deserved it a little but he would be damned if he sat here and watched her flirt with another man in his face. She was his and the sooner she knew it the better.

Tomas kissed her on both cheeks before wishing her well. Without looking in Dominic's direction, she scurried off.

Once they were alone, Tomas gave him a questioning gaze. "I didn't realize your lovely business associate and you had such close personal ties."

"Let's just say that Ms. Jackson and I go way back. Don't mind her theatrics. She can be a bit dramatic at times." Dominic held his hand up to signal the waiter over to refill his drink.

Tomas merely raised his brows as he shot Dominic a questioning gaze. He then turned to his business associates. "Gentlemen, it seems like our dinner has come to an end for the evening. If you'll excuse us, Mr. Holden and I will finish our drinks while we discuss some private matters."

The other two men nodded and said their goodbyes before leaving Dominic and Tomas alone at the table.

"I'm not sure what private matters we have to discuss, Sandoval," Dominic spoke in between sips from his refilled glass.

Unwavering dark eyes stared in his direction. A lesser man would have squirmed under that direct gaze, but Dominic didn't intimidate easily. "Have I done something to offend you, Dominic? I may call you Dominic, *si?*"

Dominic merely shrugged. "If you'd like. But to answer your first question, I'm not sure what the point of your question is."

Tomas smirked. "That's not an answer. I thought things were going along swimmingly. I'd hate to think that any future business arrangements we may have are in jeopardy because I've said or done something to cause offense."

"And I'll state again, I'm not sure why you're asking the question."

"Hmm, and here I thought you were a straight-forward man. It's one of the reasons why I was eager to work with you."

Dominic knew exactly what the other man was getting at but he wasn't about to admit it. He hated that he himself didn't understand why he was acting this way. The only thing that was certain was that he hated seeing Tomas and Krystina talking so intimately with one another, leaving him out. It fucked with his head to know that woman could get under his skin to the point where she was causing damage to potential business relationships. Already, he regretted bringing her with him. He could have easily have brought one of his assistants as he'd done in the past but he'd seen this as the perfect opportunity to set his plan in motion with Krystina.

He was probably wrong for lashing out at her the way he had, but somehow he couldn't help himself. She had the power to make him act irrationally and he hated that he'd lost his cool.

Releasing a deep breath, he looked the other man in the eyes. "No you haven't done anything to offend me and like you, I hope our negotiations work out to our mutual satisfaction."

"If I may be at liberty to say, I enjoyed the company of Ms. Jackson tonight very much and it saddened me to see that light dim in her beautiful eyes. I'm guessing there's some history between the two of you which is why you made such an ungallant statement to her. My guess is that she's more to you than you're willing to admit. I don't know your reasons and I'm not asking for them, but heed my word, *amigo*, a flower can only take so much neglect and abuse before it wilts and dies. Tend to your garden, before it's no more." Tomas stood up then. "I'll see you in the morning. Have a good night."

Left alone at the table Dominic finished the rest of his drink. He'd made a complete ass of himself but it wasn't as if he'd told a lie. Krystina was only in his life because of his grandfather's heal the world complex. But on the other hand, his outburst was inappropriate for the setting. When he saw Krystina again, he'd apologize and smooth things over.

But when he made it back to their suite, she was nowhere to be found.

Chapter Eleven

Krystina wiped angry tears from her cheeks as she walked along the beach. She was thankful that no one was out here this late. The way this resort was set up, the only people allowed on this stretch of ocean land were guests of this resort.

Just when she thought Dominic would at least be decent to her, he humiliated her again. The night had started out great with that call from Uncle Charles. And Tomas Sandoval had been a charming dinner companion. The other Sandoval associates, David and Carlos had been equally pleasant. Besides, being a great conversationalist, Tomas Sandoval was very easy on the eyes with his Mediterranean good looks. The way he'd looked at her with those dark smoldering eyes had made her giddy, like a teeny bopper at her first pop concert. He was probably quite the lady's man and she'd been flattered by his attention. But, it was nothing beyond that. Dominic had somehow ruined how she looked at other men of late. She found herself comparing other men to him and it made her feel weak to think she might actually start feeling something for a man who'd made most of her life so miserable.

But tonight, she thought things would be different. Maybe it had something to do with their interaction on the plane or perhaps she'd been caught up in the magic of the resort and city, but Krystina had believed Dominic might act like a decent human being. She'd been having so much fun at dinner that's she didn't notice that he'd remained quiet and brooding throughout the meal. And when he'd made mention of her being his grandfather's charity case, it felt as if something had broken inside of her. It wasn't like he hadn't said mean things before, but at least then, she'd been on her guard. This time around she hadn't been, and it had hurt like hell.

Krystina didn't know how she'd found the resolve to not break down and cry in front of everyone at the table, further embarrassing herself but she did. His words took her back to a time when she felt so alone in the world. She'd just lost her grandmother and she had no one to go. Shortly after her grandmother's funeral, she found Dominic and Uncle Charles arguing with each other.

Krystina was numb. Her grandmother was gone and she had no one. Who would she go home to? She had no aunts or uncles that she knew of, no slew of cousins. Her grandmother had been an only child and so was her mother. Her grandmother had died unexpectedly from a blood clot that had blocked her arteries and caused a massive heart attack. They'd only been living in the mansion for a few months and Krystina was still having trouble adjusting her to a new environment. If it weren't for her grandmother's familiar presence, she would have lost her mind.

It didn't help that the other residents in the house either ignored her or were openly hostile with the exception of Mr. Holden, who said that she could call him Uncle Charles. He was very nice but she wasn't sure if she could trust him. Yet. Her grandmother seemed to like him a lot and only had nice things to say about him.

And now, she was gone. Krystina felt like she was living outside her body the entire day of the funeral. She didn't know how she'd gotten dressed or how she even got to the church where the service had been held. All that she could remember was that she'd been surrounded by a roomful of strangers and the lifeless body in the coffin that they said was her grandmother.

Krystina didn't even remember the repast where well-wishers she didn't know offered their condolences. One thing that did stick out, however, was Ms. Lakes. The woman had stayed in the back of the church and she seemed to have this gleam of satisfaction in her eyes. It seemed so out of place for a funeral, but Krystina didn't really think too much of it because she'd been too wrapped up in her own pain.

When everyone returned to the mansion, she'd gone to her grandmother's room and curled up on the bed the old woman used to sleep on, inhaling the scent that still lingered. She must have drifted off because when she woke up, it was dark and her throat felt like sandpaper. Needing a drink to relieve the ache in her throat, she headed downstairs toward the kitchen and heard raised voices in the family room. She wasn't sure what compelled her to go in the direction of that sound but curiosity got the better of her.

"I don't care who her mother or grandmother was. You have no further obligation to that girl. Send her to foster care of something." The voice belonged to Dominic and she was certain, he was talking about her.

Krystina's heart seized in her chest as she hugged the wall so that she wouldn't be detected.

"The place where she belongs is here. I made a promise to her grandmother to look out for her and it's one, I intend to keep. I don't know what the hell has gotten into you, but I think you've forgotten who the hell you're talking to. I suggest you watch your tone, boy. I may be an old man but if you speak to me like that again, I will make you rue the day. Do you understand me?" That voice definitely belonged to Mr. Holden.

"Speak up, Dominic, I didn't quite hear you."

"Yes, sir."

"That's better."

"Look, I mean no disrespect but what's she doing here anyway? She doesn't belong. Can't you just send her back where she came from?"

"She has no other relatives and don't you dare bring up sending her to foster care again because that's out of the question."

"What about her father? Everyone has one. Maybe if you found him, you could pay him to take her off your hands."

"With the kind of life her mother lived up until her birth, her father could be anyone. Not that it matters. She's now my responsibility. I failed Willie Mae and Candice but I'll be damned if I fail that little girl, too. You need to start showing her a little charity. The two of you have a lot in common. Maybe if you stopped blaming her for something she had no control over, you'd see how unreasonable you're being. She's a child!"

"We're nothing alike. This is my family and whether she stays here or not, I will never accept her as one of us."

"Dominic!"

Krystina was taken by surprise when the nineteen-year-old came storming out of the room. He was so focused on leaving the room that he didn't notice her when he passed by.

Her heart literally hurt after that exchange. She didn't cry during the funeral or even when she'd learned of her grandmother's death because everything had seemed so surreal. But now, she found herself collapsing to the ground as a round of body-shaking sobs ripped through her entire being. She didn't understand why Dominic hated her so much but today served as a reminder to just how alone in this world she was.

She didn't know how long she walked on the beach. By the time she was finished, she was all cried out and exhausted. As she headed back to the resort, she saw a figure standing near the entrance, watching her. She stiffened as she got closer and discovered it was Dominic. Hands in pocket, a stoic expression rested on his face.

Krystina was prepared to walk past him but he said her name so softly, she thought she might have imagined it.

"Krystina."

With a heavy sigh, she turned to face him. "What do you want, Dominic? It's late and I'm in no mood to argue."

"I'm not out here to argue. I wanted to make you sure you were all right."

She shrugged. "Well, as you can see, I'm all in one piece. You can leave me alone now."

"Wait. I uh… also wanted to apologize. What I said was out of line."

"Accepted. Can I go?"

"I mean it, Krystina."

"What difference does your apology make? You'll just say something as equally fucked up, eventually. It seems to be the cycle. You say something foul. I say something back. We avoid each other and then, the pattern continues. Look, let's just get through these next seven days with the least amount of conflict as possible."

"How can we, when you're ignoring the immediate issue between us? Neither one of us will be able to move on, unless we address the elephant in the room."

She rolled her eyes. "And what might that be?"

"The sexual tension between us is so thick, you can cut it with a knife. I want you, Krystina. I won't lie about that, but you need to stop lying to yourself."

She took a step away from him, realizing where this was heading. If she wasn't careful, she'd find herself on her back with Dominic between her legs. "Just stop it.

Why should I have sex with you, when all you do is put me down every chance you get?

"Because every single time I've had you in my arms, you had the opportunity to say no, but you never do. Why is that? Yes, I was an asshole tonight but—"

She snorted. "You're an asshole every night."

He gritted his teeth. "As I was saying, I may have been an asshole, but it doesn't change the fact that I want you and I will have you, once and for all."

"You can't be serious."

"I've never been more serious in my life. You may pretend that this isn't going to happen, but I'm not going to."

Krystina wanted to scream in frustration. There had to be some kind of disconnect in Dominic's head that made him put her down one second and then come on to her in the next. It was such crazy behavior. Maybe she was the insane one because right now, all she could think about was how she'd felt when he had her stretched out over his desk.

In that second, she had an epiphany. She was going to give him what he wanted. She might regret it in the morning; but right now, she was tired of this tightness in her chest. In this moment Krystina, would do anything to ease the pain and if that meant having sex with Dominic, then so be it.

She lifted her head to meet his gaze. "Ok."

His brows shot up and it seemed as if her words took him by surprise. "Okay, what?"

"You want me? Then, have me."

He gripped her forearms in each of his hands and yanked her against the hard wall of his chest. "You better not be messing with me, because once I get you into my bed there's no turning back."

She nodded. "I know."

Without another word, he took her hand and practically dragged her behind him. Krystina had to practically jog to keep up with his long strides. And when they finally got back to their suite, Dominic scooped her into his arms and carried her to his room. He tossed her on the middle of the king-sized bed with enough force to take her breath away. Before she had a chance to recover, he crashed on top of her.

Dominic placed a bruising kiss on her lips. He kissed her with the savagery of a thirsty man in desperate need of a drink. "Open your mouth so I can taste you properly."

Krystina parted her lips and welcomed the forceful invasion of his tongue. She could taste the cognac he'd consumed earlier and it gave her a dizzying feeling. As his tongue explored her mouth, his hands roamed her body. They slid along her sides, grazing her breasts and hips.

Without warning, he rolled off of Krystina and knelt beside her. His eyes had darkened to the point where, if she didn't know any better she would think, they were dark green instead of their usual aqua shade. "You've been teasing me all night, making me want you. Your tits were on display for everyone to see and you were driving us all crazy. Every single man at that table wanted you, but I'm the only one who gets to touch these tonight." He caught her dress with both hands and ripped it down the front. Her boobs came tumbling out because the dress had a built-in bra.

"My dress!" she exclaimed in surprise.

"Fuck this dress. I'll buy you more. But as I was saying, I'm the only one who does this." He squeezed her globes in his palms none too gently. To her shame, her nipples puckered beneath his touch. She arched her back, wanting more. Dominic obliged, kneading and shaping them. She moaned with pleasure as desire coursed throughout her being.

"And I'm damn sure going to be the only one to do this." He dipped his head and captured a turgid tip in his mouth, and begin to nibble and suck. Krystina threaded her fingers through his dark hair, holding his head against her chest as he used his mouth to do the most amazing things. He circled her nipple with the tip of his tongue, licking and laving it, sending flashes of heat to her core.

Dominic transferred his attention to her other breast and gave it the same attention, wetting it with his mouth. He ran a wet trail down the center of her body with his mouth stopping to pay homage to her navel. He dipped his tongue inside of her making her shiver in delight. Krystina had had lovers before but never did she think something so simple could be so erotic. Then, he slowly removed her panties and brought them to his nose. Dominic inhaled deeply. "Your scent gets me high."

Krystina never thought she'd be so turned on at the sight of someone sniffing her panties, but seeing Dominic doing it made her already wet pussy drip. She released a low moan, not trusting herself to speak.

Instead of diving in, like she thought Dominic would, he raised his head to catch her gaze. "And no one is going to be tasting this pussy tonight, except me. But I'm warning you right now, duchess, I'm not going to stop once I finish eating your pussy. I'm going to fuck you tonight so you'll never forget who you belong to. So if you don't want this, you better speak up now."

All that she managed to get out was a weak whimper.

"Tell me to stop," he commanded softly.

With a sigh, she finally whispered. "I don't want you to."

"Damn right you don't," he growled before turning his attention to her warm center. He parted her tender pussy lips and bumped his nose against her clit before blowing on it. "I love how your pussy comes to life at the least bit of stimulation. So wet and beautiful. Is all this for me, duchess?"

Krystina bit her bottom lip to stop herself from crying out. What was it about this man that made her so sexually indebted to him? She couldn't reconcile how she could hate him one minute and then want him the next.

To her surprise, he gave her pussy a smack with her clit taking the brunt of the force. "Answer me, when I ask you a question. Is this all for me?" He smacked her cunt again and she nearly lost it right then and there.

"Yes! It's all for you. Please, stop teasing me."

"I want you to beg for it."

"I..I..please."

He spanked her pussy in rapid succession making her flinch and cry out. It hurt like hell, but still felt good at the same time. "Not good enough."

"Please, eat my pussy. I want your mouth on me," she cried. The pleasure pain, sent her reeling so close to the edge of a powerful climax.

Dominic chuckled. "Well, since you asked nicely." He swiped her sore pussy with his tongue, taking his time exploring every bit of her from her inner and outer labia. He slipped his middle finger into her channel and eased it in and out of her before taking her clit into his mouth. He sucked gently at first but then he grew more aggressive, pumping in and out of her with more force and tightening his lips around her throbbing little button.

Unable to hold back any longer, she was hurtled into a powerful climax.

"Oh, God, yes!" She lifted her hips and mashed her sex against his face. Dominic hungrily latched on, slurping up her juices. As she floated from the cloud that she'd soared to, he slowly slipped his finger out of her and pulled away from her.

"Don't move a muscle," he commanded. He kept his gaze focused on her as he quickly removed his clothing.

Krystina couldn't move, even if she wanted to. Each item of clothing he removed, revealed a hard toned body. The tall slender frame beneath his expensive suits belied a frame that was ripped with corded muscles. He had tight well-developed pecs and a flat washboard stomach that made it clear that he took good care of his body. Her eyes drifted lower to reveal his cock which was hard and long. It wasn't the biggest she'd ever seen, but he it was slightly above average and beautifully formed. What made his burgeoning member stand out was how thick it was, making her wonder if that thing would fit inside of her.

He wrapped his fist around his cock and stroked himself. "Play with your tits."

Krystina hesitated, mesmerized by the motion of his hand sliding up and down his member.

"Now,' he growled.

She cupped her breasts in her palms and squeezed them. She moaned as she ran the pad of her thumbs over her nipples. Heat licked every nerve ending within her, threatening to send her body bursting into flames. His heated gaze on her body was driving her insane. If he didn't take her now, Krystina thought she'd lose her mind. "I need you."

Dominic licked his lips and grinned. "You don't have to tell me again, duchess. I'm all yours." Moving to the bed, he tore away what was left of her dress and pushed her legs apart. He settled himself between her thighs and placed his cock against her slick entrance. "There's no going back after this, duchess."

"I know. I'm ready."

Chapter Twelve

Hearing her whisper those words, was like a blessing from heaven. Finally, she would be his in every sense of the word. Unable to hold back a second longer, he pushed through her tight box with one powerful thrust.

"Oh, God! Dominic!" She cried out.

Dominic inhaled sharply. "So fucking tight. Damn. How did I go this long without experiencing this pussy?" He could barely get the words out. Her walls were squeezing the shit out of his cock and he didn't think he could hold on for very long. It would take a considerable amount of will to not spill his seed right now.

She whimpered beneath him and wiggled. "I'm so full. Too much."

"You'll adjust. Just take it easy, duchess. I'll make it good for you." With one hand holding him braced above her quivering frame, he moved his other hand between her legs and started to circle her clit with his finger. Slowly, he could feel her muscles relax.

"Mmm," she moaned.

"Ready?"

"Yes."

He pulled his cock out of her pussy until only the head remained and then he shoved it back into the hilt. Dominic repeated the motion. He loved the way her eyes lit up with wonder and passion as he moved within her. He couldn't remember a time when he'd been with a woman who made him nearly lose it from the first stroke. He hadn't felt this way since he was an untrained virgin.

As he continued to move, he lowered himself to kiss her sweat-dampened brow. She was so beautiful and she was all his.

"Dominic," she whispered. "I'm so close."

"Then don't hold back. Come for me."

He didn't think it was possible but she clenched her walls around his cock even tighter than before. He completely lost all control and shot his seed deep inside of her.

She wrapped her legs around his waist and she pulled him deeper still. He buried his face against her shoulder. Krystina drug her nails down his back as he collapsed on top of her.

Dominic wrapped his arms around her and rolled over with her until Krystina rested on his chest. He stroked the back of her head trying to figure out what this sensation was that he was feeling. He didn't quite know what it was but he kind of liked it. It felt good to hold her like this. "Are you okay?"

She didn't say anything.

"Krystina?"

"What?"

"I asked if you were okay."

"I'm fine. I'm just trying to process what happened."

"What's to process? We had sex and we both enjoyed it."

"Hmm."

"Is that all you have to say?"

"What do you want me to say, Dominic?"

"Well, I expected more than just a 'hmm'."

"You got what you wanted from me, isn't that enough?"

"Oh, duchess, it's not nearly enough. This is only the beginning."

She didn't respond.

"No argument?"

"What's the point of arguing about it? It's clear the two of us are sexually attracted to each other and we'll probably do it again. I just didn't expect you to want to make a big deal about it afterward." The coolness of her tone took him by surprise. He wanted to keep feelings out of this, but hearing how detached she was didn't sit well with him for some reason.

A thought suddenly occurred to him. "Shit. We didn't use anything."

Krystina, however, seemed unconcerned. "Relax. I'm on birth control. Have been since college."

That should have made him feel better, but somehow it didn't.

She rolled out of his arms and slid off the bed, giving him a view of her scrumptious backside. Her hair had broken free from its band and it was wild and bed-tussled. Dominic could feel himself getting hard again and he had the urge to pull her back into his arms and take her again but something stopped him. "Where are you going?"

"It's late and I'm tired. We have to get up early tomorrow. I need to shower and go to bed."

It was on the tip of his tongue to invite her to sleep with him in his bed but he thought better of it. "Make sure you dress appropriately tomorrow."

She stiffened briefly before picking her tattered dress off the ground and walking out of his room. Krystina closed the door behind her with a decisive click. Now that he finally had her that should have been the end of it. Instead, now he wanted her even more, making him wonder if he would ever be able to work her out of his system.

Krystina was exhausted when her alarm had gone off. Despite being tired when she'd gone to bed, she didn't get a lot of sleep. She'd tossed and turned most of the night, thinking about how she'd completely surrendered to Dominic, the man she had vowed to hate. But the thing that sucked the most was that she didn't really hate him. Maybe she never did. She'd been a girl without a family among a bunch of strangers. In those first few months after her grandmother had died, Krystina could admit that she was anti-social and angry all the time. She had, after all, gone through a traumatic experience and had lost her closest relative.

But as time passed and she grew closer to her guardian, Krystina had wanted more than anything to fit in and feel like she belonged. She realized then that if she was to become a real member of their family, she'd have to get into Dominic's good graces. So whenever he'd come home from school, she made it a point to be as nice as she could to him. But no matter how hard she tried, he'd rebuffed her every step of the way. She finally got the hint when he'd uttered those words that she took to heart. *You will never belong.*

That had been the turning point for her where Dominic was concerned. But even when she thought she hated him, she never really did. And now she was in this predicament. She wasn't the type of person to go in for casual sex. All three of her previous lovers were men she'd had some type of feelings for. Her first lover was in college. Jeremiah was an aspiring spoken word artist with dreadlocks down his back and beautiful caramel eyes. He'd been a gentle lover and he was the first guy she thought herself to be in love with. They'd been together for nearly a year when Jeremiah decided he needed space. Krystina had been heartbroken but she'd moved on.

Though she'd dated here and there throughout college, she didn't have another serious boyfriend until her first trip to Paris where she met Francois. He owned a coffee shop she'd frequented. Francois was a master with his hands and tongue, but she soon found she wasn't the only girl he was using that tongue on. Her last boyfriend was Kevin. A South African native she'd done volunteer work with. Kevin had been okay, but looking back, she honestly couldn't remember much about their sexual encounters. Eventually, they both realized they were better off being friends.

Sex was something she could take or leave, before now. Dominic had done things to her that she'd only ever read in dirty books. Her encounters with Jeremiah, Francois and Kevin hadn't prepared her for Dominic, who seemed to know all the spots to hit to make her body sing with desire. No one had made her ache quite the way he did. Something about the way he took her when they were intimate, turned Krystina on.

Still, she couldn't understand how out of all the men in the world, why did it have to be Dominic who'd awaken something in her that made her react in ways that she couldn't understand. She'd shared her body with him which had meant something to her. They'd made a connection and for that, they would always be tied together somehow in the metaphysical sense. Perhaps, that little girl who had desperately wanted his approval at one time in her life wasn't completely gone. But for whatever reason, she was now a prisoner of her own sexual needs.

It took a lot of energy to drag herself out of bed that morning to get dressed. When she left her room, she was hit with the scent of cinnamon and fresh baked bread. She walked into the dining room to see a spread of a traditional Spanish breakfast of churros, hot chocolate, magdelenas, bread with tomato, potato omelets, fruit and various spreads. Dominic was already at the table scrolling through his tablet. He looked up when she entered the room and nodded in her direction. "Good morning."

"Morning," she mumbled. "I didn't realize you'd ordered breakfast." She took the seat across from him and took a plate. She wasn't particularly hungry but the food looked amazing and she didn't want it all to go to waste. She took one of the churros and a handful of grapes.

"I didn't. Javier set it up for us based on our wake up time." He eyed her plate. "I hope you intend to eat more than that. We're in for a long day. Sandoval will be showing us around his operation today and he'll be going over the plan for how our potential partnership will work."

"I'm pacing myself." Krystina kept her attention focused on her food. After taking a few bites, she realized she was hungrier than she'd originally thought and placed an omelet on her plate.

"Krystina."

She raised her head to look at him. "What?"

"About last night…"

"What about it? You got what you wanted."

"Not by a long shot duchess, this is only the beginning. What I was going to say is that I think it's best if you keep things on a professional level with Tomas Sandoval. Remember, we're here on business."

She refused to let him bait her this early in the morning. Krystina wasn't going to allow Satan to win today. She stuffed her mouth with a magdelena to keep back the angry retort on her tongue. He had a lot of nerve questioning her professionalism when he'd humiliated her in front of those men last night.

"Are we understood?"

She continued to chew as slowly as she possibly could. Krystina then made a show out of pouring a glass of guava juice and taking a sip from it.

"Krystina," Dominic said her name with a low growl.

"I'm not sure what you'd like me to say to that. You say that we're here on business and you imply that I was less than professional last night when you were the one who couldn't keep his hands to himself."

"That was different?"

"Oh? How is that? Are you saying the rules don't apply to the great Dominic Holden?"

"I'm saying that I'm very possessive over what is mine and as long as I want you, you're mine, and if I see you flirting with Sandoval today, I'm going to put you over my knee and tear that ass up."

His words should have pissed her off more than they actually did. Instead, she found herself squirming in her seat. Her panties started to get damp from just the thought of his palm crashing on her ass and then alternately caressing it. What the hell was wrong with her? When did she become such a masochist?

"Are we clear?"

"As crystal."

Krystina didn't know how she would get through the rest of this trip without losing her mind, dignity and most of all her heart.

Chapter Thirteen

She was doing it again, and it was ticking him off. Each time she laughed at one of Sandoval's dry jokes, he added it to the number of licks he planned on giving her. Krystina had remained in the background for most of the meeting, not saying anything during the entire presentation. She only took notes as directed.

But after the meeting when they had lunch, she sat next to the Spanish businessman giving him that smile he now resented the hell out of. He didn't want to call this jealousy because he'd never been jealous of anyone. He was simply pissed that she couldn't follow simple instructions. To compound her transgressions, they'd taken a tour later that day on one of the estates Sandoval owned that Dominic was interested in using as part of his own tour packet for the resort. During the ride, Dominic had sat in the front of the all-terrain vehicle with the driver while Krystina sat in the back in between Sandoval and one of the associates from last night's dinner.

He was going to spank that ass good and then fuck her until she couldn't walk straight. It was like she was doing it deliberately. It didn't help matters that they were speaking in Spanish and Dominic only had a rudimentary understanding of the language. At one point, he caught Krystina's gaze in the rear view mirror. She quickly looked away from him, probably because she knew she would get it later on that night, literally and figuratively.

As they toured the estate, to Dominic's further frustration, he noticed how the other man continually found ways to touch Krystina and she didn't seem to mind one bit. Dominic asked the occasional question, but for the most part he kept his thoughts to himself.

Dominic clenched his fists at his sides when he saw Krystina place her hand on Sandoval's shoulder. *"Donde esta el baño? Necesito refrescarme."*

*"Te mostraré."*Sandoval smiled before turning to Dominic. "If you'll excuse us, I'll show the lady to the restroom."

"I understood," Dominic responded. He could feel the vein throbbing in his forehead. He was almost certain they were fucking with him deliberately at this point.

He watched the two of them go in the other direction and he was on the verge of following them, but he had to remind himself that this was business. Instead of focusing on those two, he asked questions of the other two associates that were with them. A few minutes later, Sandoval returned without Krystina. "Your lovely colleague will rejoin us shortly. Shall we continue the tour?"

Dominic wanted to punch the smug grin off the other man's face. "Actually, would you mind telling me where the restroom is? I'd rather wait until Ms. Jackson has returned before we resume."

"Oh, of course. Shall I show you?"

"If you tell me where it is, I think I'll be able to find it."

The other man raised a questioning brow before shrugging. "You need to go down the hall, make a left and you'll see a set stairwell. Go up the stairs and turn right and it will be the first door on the left. That's one of the private quarters that will be off limits to tourists but I use that area of the house whenever I'm here," Sandoval explained.

"Thank you. I'll return shortly."

"Take your time. We'll wait for you in the sitting room where I believe the staff has prepared refreshments for us."

Dominic nodded in acknowledgment. He took the directions he was given and entered a room that seemed to be its own self-contained apartment with a kitchen, sitting room area and bedroom. He heard water running in one of the rooms which must have been the bathroom. He stood outside the door and waited. Sure enough, not even a minute later, Krystina walked out. She jumped in obvious surprise. "Dominic! What are you doing up here?"

He was already angry but the fact that she was playing the innocent only served to set him off even more. Without a word, he pushed her back into the bathroom and closed the door behind him.

"What the hell are you doing?" She cried out taking several steps back until she was trapped between his body and the sink.

"I fucking told you what would happen if you flirted with Sandoval today."

Her eyes grew as big as saucers. "Are you kidding me? I wasn't flirting. I was being friendly with him and asking questions related to the job. Isn't that what you wanted?"

"Being friendly doesn't require you giggling and batting those beautiful brown eyes at him. You let that motherfucker touch you over and over and now, you're going to have to pay the price."

"What are you doing?"

He turned her around and bent her over the sink. She stiffened for a moment but then she began to buck and fight against him as if her life depended on it. "Get off of me! What the hell is wrong with you?"

Ignoring her protests, he held her in place and hiked up her skirt and yanked down her panties. He brought his palm down on her rear in rapid succession giving her absolutely no mercy. All he could see was the other man's hands on her and he didn't like it one bit.

"Stop, Dominic!" She tried to thrust him off but he wouldn't be moved.

"This is what happens when you don't listen, Krystina."

All while he was spanking her, he was mesmerized by the ripples in her bottom that his hand caused whenever it would connect with it. She had a nice firm ass but he liked the way it bounced on impact. His dick was so hard right now he desperately needed relief.

He wrapped one hand around her throat and gave it a slight squeeze while fumbling with the button and zipper on his pants. Once his cock was free, he guided it to her wet entrance and slammed into her. He then put his other hand around her neck and began to aggressively pump in and out of her. No words were spoken. Only frantic, grunts and moans were exchanged.

Krystina grasped the sink, holding herself up as he continued to pummel into her. Every time he went deep, he'd squeeze her neck just a little bit tighter. Her walls had his dick in a vice, clenching him so snuggly he was pushed to a quick climax. Letting go of her neck, he gripped her hips as he shot his seed deep inside her core. Only when he'd released every single drop of his essence did he pull back.

He then shoved his cock back into his pants and fixed his clothes. Krystina remained hunched over the sink, her breathing ragged. Dominic wasn't finished with his lesson yet, however. He pushed his finger into her dripping cunt making her gasp out loud. He wiggled the digit around for several seconds until it was thoroughly coated with a mixture of his cum and her juices. Then he brought the finger to her mouth and pushed it past her lips.

"This is what I want you to keep in mind for the rest of the day. When you're talking to him, it's me that you're tasting and it's my cum in that tight little pussy of yours. When you can't sit down because your bottom is sore, you'll think of me. And do you know why, duchess? It's because you belong to me. Don't forget it."

After wiping his fingers on a hand towel, he looked in the mirror to make sure his appearance was in order before leaving Krystina at the sink.

Dominic found Sandoval and the other two associates in the sitting area like he said they'd be. Sandoval frowned. "Where's Krystina?"

"Ms. Jackson isn't feeling very well. She'll just be a moment."

"I see," was all the other man said.

For the first time since the day began, Dominic was in a good mood.

<><><><><>

He'd done it again and what was worse, she'd loved every second of it. Every sexual encounter they had, Dominic managed to push her boundaries a little further. She'd heard of erotic asphyxiation, but she never thought it would be such a turn on. For the life of her, she couldn't figure out what was the matter with her. How could she like this when he clearly didn't value her beyond what was between her legs? How much more punishment would she be able to handle before she reached her breaking point?

Sometimes, it felt like he was punishing her for something she had no control over and she didn't know what it was. This was only their second day in Spain and already she was nearly broken. Maybe she'd sensed something like this could happen to her all along which was why she'd fled three years ago. Dominic seemed to have some kind of weird control over her that she couldn't explain.

She wasn't sure how long she stood in front of the seat, her arms had stiffened and her knees felt week. She plopped down on the toilet and grabbed a tissue to wipe away the trail of moisture dribbling down her thighs. As she cleaned herself up, she grew angry and as each second passed, she grew even more perturbed. It didn't matter that she'd been turned on; she couldn't allow him to keep treating her like this. She wasn't his plaything that he could just use as he saw fit. But, she was really upset with herself. How would she fight him off the next time he touched her or had her back against the wall? No didn't mean a damn thing to him and most of the time, she said it half-heartedly.

If nothing else, this trip was making it quite clear that working for Dominic just wasn't going to work out. When they went back home, she'd have to hand in her resignation and hope that Dominic had a shred of decency not to show his grandfather the picture of her in his office. She'd just have to play his game for the rest of the week but she'd get through this. She was a survivor.

She'd weathered many storms in her twenty-three years. She'd make it through Hurricane Dominic. She hoped.

By the time she'd gotten her appearance in order and made it back downstairs, the group wasn't in the same spot where she'd left them but there was a man dressed in a gray suit waiting for her. He directed her to a lounge where the rest of the group was waiting. Dominic eyed her with an unreadable expression in his aqua gaze. She wanted to punch him in his handsome face because even now, after what he'd done to her, Krystina could feel her temperature rise. Her butt was still warm from the spanking he'd given her and just as he'd predicted, she didn't want to sit down.

"Krystina." Tomas stood when she entered the room as did the rest of the men, except for Dominic who continued to silently stare. "I trust everything is okay with you. Your boss mentioned that you weren't feeling well."

"I, uh, yeah. I sometimes get these dizzy spells. This Spanish heat takes some getting used to. But thank you for asking, Mr. Sandoval."

Tomas raised a brow in question at her formal reply. He'd insisted that she call him by his first name which she did, but her being friendly toward him actually seemed to set Dominic off and she wanted to avoid any further conflict for the rest of the trip if she could.

"Perhaps, you'd like a drink or to partake in this delicious spread my chef has prepared."

"Um, thank you. I think I will, but no thank you to the drink." Avoiding eye contact, she walked over to the table that had finger sandwiches and appetizer like snacks. It was a lot of food for only five people but the one thing she'd learned about dealing with the super wealthy was that they lived superfluous lives. Though she wasn't really hungry, she took a couple of finger sandwiches, more so to keep herself occupied. She decided the less she talked, the better.

Krystina took the empty space on the couch next to Dominic.

For the remainder of their time there, the men talked business and Krystina only half listened to the conversation. Every now and then, Tomas would try to draw her into the discussion but she would smile politely and answer with the fewest words possible without being rude.

On the way back to the resort, she took the seat in front while the men sat in back. With their business concluded for the day, Krystina made a beeline for her suite and immediately went to her room to shower but no matter how much she scrubbed her body, she could still smell him. All she could think about was his hands on her body and how she almost missed him.

Almost. She didn't think she could deal with him right now. For her own peace of mind, she needed a break from him.

Once her toiletry was complete, she dressed in her nightshirt and slid into bed. She drifted off the second her head hit the pillow.

She was only eleven. Too young to die. There was so much she wanted to see and do. She'd never even left her hometown before. Krystina wondered if they'd find her body drifting in a pool of water like she'd seen before on television. Grandma didn't look well. They'd been stuck here for three days and she'd missed her dialysis appointment and her insulin was gone. The little food that they'd managed to take to the attic with them was nearly gone. And yet, it continued to rain. "I'm scared Grandma," she whispered hugging her knees to her chest. The coastal Mississippi home that she and her grandmother shared had been hit by hurricanes before, but nothing like the likes of this. When the weatherman had said this would be the big one, no one paid any mind to the doom and gloom report because they'd heard it all before. Whenever there was a report of a severe tropical storm or hurricane, the neighborhood threw barbecues and block parties because, for all the blustering of the weather reports, there was usually just a few inches of rain, and minor property damage. But no one had been prepared for the likes of this disaster. Despite the Governor calling for an evacuation of the area, no one listened. Where would they go after all? Most people didn't have the money to simply up and leave.

Not only did the storm cause a cataclysmic amount of damage with street signs being knocked down, roofs caving in and windows shattered. On top of that, one of the levees that kept the water at bay malfunctioned and a huge sinkhole had opened up taking several houses with it. One of those houses had belonged to Krystina's best friend, Tasha. Now, Krystina feared she was next. The water levels were rising and it wouldn't be long before it reached the attic where she and her grandmother had taken shelter.

When the firemen had come a few days ago, they had the opportunity to go to the local high school for shelter which was above water level but her grandmother distrusted them for some reason which is how they found themselves in the attic, waiting to die. Krystina wondered if she would see her mother.

"I'm scared, too, child." Her grandmother finally answered.

The admission took Krystina by surprise. Her grandmother was her fearless rock who she clung to in times of uncertainty. If Grandma was scared, where did that leave Krystina?

"Are we going to die?" She dared to say out loud what had been on her mind for the past couple days.

"We'll go when it's our time. Just...keep faith, child."

Krystina slid close to the old woman and allowed herself to be engulfed in her embrace. She must have fallen asleep because when she opened her eyes again, the sound from outside had changed. Instead of the steady beating of rain on the rooftop, she heard the sound of a motor. She raised her head from her grandmother's chest. "Grandma? What's that sound?"

Willie Mae's eyes remained closed. Krystina's heart fell. She shook the older woman in hopes of getting some kind of response but she remained unresponsive.

"Grandma!" she screamed in a panic. The body was still warm so that was at least something. When Krystina had touched her mother's body in the coffin, it had been ice cold. This had to mean something.

Maybe it was her blood sugar? She looked around the room for something she could give her grandmother to eat. The only thing remaining were two stale pieces of bread. In her panicked state, Krystina noticed the sound of the motor getting closer and then as if the voice of God himself spoke, she heard,

"Anyone still in your home, please give us a signal."

The voice had come from outside. She ran to the window and saw two men in orange vests on a big boat. Krystina attempted to open the window but it was stuck. She had to get their attention so that they could save her grandmother. Desperately, she searched the room for something she could shatter the glass with and her gaze fell on a coat hanger. She lifted the sturdy wooden apparatus and shoved it against the window with all her might. The glass cracked a little at first, but then she hit it again and it finally broke into tiny pieces. "Help!" she screamed through the now empty pane.

It felt like an eternity before the boat came in her direction. One of the men reached out to her and she was about to take his hand but she tripped and fell into the puddle of water. She kept sinking and no matter how hard she struggled, she kept drowning.

Chapter Fourteen

Dominic woke to the sound of screaming. Disoriented at first, he wasn't sure if it was real or if he was imagining it, not until the sound grew more deafening. Krystina! He slipped out of bed and raced out the room. Sure enough, when he got to her door, he could hear her cries.

"Help!' she screamed.

Her door was locked.

Dominic threw his body against the door to break it open, but it didn't budge. He kicked it with the heel of his foot the next time. He kept kicking until he heard the lock give. Only then was he able to shove the door open. He turned on the light and found Krystina crying and thrashing on the bed. When he reached out to her, she fought him but he captured her wrists in one of his hands and gave her cheek a light tap to wake her gently. "Krystina. Wake up."

She continued to struggle for a few more seconds before opening her eyes. She blinked several times as if she was trying to figure out whether or not she was still dreaming. "Dominic? What are you doing here?"

"You were screaming the place down. I came in here to see what was going on. What was that all about?"

She pulled her wrists out of his grip and scooted away. "I...it was nothing. I'm sorry for disturbing you. You can go back to sleep now."

He frowned. "Like hell, it was nothing. You don't scream bloody murder like that and it be absolutely nothing. Tell me, what was your dream about?"

"Why are you so interested?"

"Because someone doesn't scream like that unless something is wrong."

"It's not your concern."

"It is when it wakes me up in the middle of the night."

"I'm sorry. Don't worry about it, okay?

He was trying very hard to be patient with her in her state of obvious distress but she was slowly starting to wear on his patience. It was bad enough that she'd completely disappeared when they'd returned to the resort. He'd intended to have a special meal prepared for her as a way to offer an olive branch. He had been a complete monster. It was his way of apologizing for ambushing her in the bathroom. He'd let his emotions get the better of him and while he didn't regret taking her and claiming every inch of that sweet pussy, he wished he would have refrained until they weren't in the middle of a business meeting. "Krystina, just tell me. I wouldn't have come in here if I wasn't interested. I care because you're obviously upset."

"It was just a bad dream. Everyone has them."

"Not like that. There was real terror in your voice. I haven't heard anything like that since..." he trailed off with a frown. He had heard that scream before. When Krystina was younger. One night he woke up to hear her screaming bloody murder. He'd raced to her room as did the rest of the residents who had been awakened by the ruckus. His grandfather had shooed everyone back to bed, saying that he would handle it. Dominic remembered the old man holding a sobbing Krystina. At the time, he thought it was just her angling for attention but looking back, he realized that was an unfair assessment. How long had she been suffering from these night terrors and why hadn't his grandfather ever said anything about it to him before? "You used to have dreams like that when you were a child, didn't you?

"I haven't had this dream in years. I'm not sure why it came back tonight all of a sudden."

"Do you have different nightmares or was it just one in particular?"

"It's always been the same one."

"Tell me about it."

She glanced at him with wariness shadowing her eyes.

He took her hand and gave it a gentle pat. "I know we haven't always seen eye to eye but I'm here to listen if you need to get something off your chest."

Krystina sighed. "Fine. It was the dream of when me and my grandmother lost our home. It was during the storm."

Dominic nodded. The hurricane that had devastated the coastal gulf area was the reason Krystina and Miss Willie Mae had come to live with them. His grandfather had read about the storm's effect in the newspaper and had sent someone to look into how his former housekeeper, who had moved down to that area, was faring. That's when Charles had found out that Miss Willie Mae and her granddaughter were homeless. That storm had changed Dominic's life but he kept his thoughts about it to himself.

"It must have been a traumatizing experience."

She nodded. "My entire street was wiped out. No one took the storm seriously because meteorologists get it wrong all the time. We didn't think this storm would be any different and no one in my area evacuated like they were supposed to but the thing was, most of us had nowhere to go except to the high school. My grandmother didn't have a car and relied on friends and a local service for the elderly to get around town. A lot of people in my area didn't have vehicles and our public transportation system which already sucked had completely shut down."

Dominic remembered hearing about the people who didn't leave their homes when they'd been given the opportunity. At the time, he thought the people who got caught in the storm got what was coming to them for not listening to the warning. He hadn't bothered seeing it from another perspective. "It must have been pretty scary."

"It wasn't at first. We never took those types of things serious because we'd dealt with hurricanes before but this one happened to be the one we should have looked out for."

"I understand you and your grandmother had lost everything. What exactly happened? Grandfather mentioned something about you being rescued. Did your dream have anything to do with that?"

"Sort of. It rained for days, it felt like we were in the middle of Noah's Ark. The roads started to flood and a huge sinkhole opened up a few houses down from us. And then one of the levees malfunctioned and that made things so much worse. The water was as high as some houses. Me and Grandma couldn't swim so we gathered up some food and water and stayed in the attic for a few days. The water started coming into our house fast and we realized too late that we'd left Grandma's insulin in the fridge. I was so worried about her. She was weak and she'd nod in an out. Whenever she would drift off, I'd check to make sure she was still breathing. Because of the storm, she couldn't go to her dialysis appointment which made matters even worse. We had to urinate in a bucket and we were unable to bathe. I was certain we were going to die. The last day we were in the attic, I had fallen asleep in my grandma's arms. When I opened my eyes, she seemed so still. I tried to wake her up but she wouldn't. And then, I heard it. The men in boats were going by people's homes, and pulling people off their roofs and getting them out of their attics. But, I thought she was going to die. The men came into the window I broke to call out to them. They took my grandmother and me to the hospital and thankfully Grandma pulled through but in my dream, when I'm reaching out to the men, I somehow slip and fall into the water and I'm drowning. Every time I open my mouth to scream, no words come out because the water is filling my lungs and I'm drowning. That part didn't actually happen though but the other stuff did."

"The other stuff sounds scary enough. I'm really sorry that you went through that. I had no idea."

She shrugged. "How could you have known? You weren't exactly interested in getting to know about me when I showed up. You seemed to like my grandmother well enough."

Dominic raked his fingers through his hair. "You're right. I was dealing with a lot of stuff when you and your grandmother came to live with us. I don't think I would have appreciated anyone's intrusion but I was respectful toward your grandmother because I remember her being my grandfather's housekeeper when I was younger and coming to his house for a visit. At the time, my grandfather lived in a smaller house since it was just him. Your grandmother was always nice to me. She could be very outspoken at times, though."

Krystina smiled. "She had a way of putting a person in their place one minute and giving that same person a hug the next. She was quite a character."

Dominic grinned as well. "She was one of the few people Ms. Lakes was actually scared of. Your grandmother had to tell her off a few times."

"You never did say why you guys let her go. I just came home from boarding school one break and she was gone. I thought she'd be around forever. But to be perfectly honest, I'm glad she was gone. She made my existence miserable. Always taking shots at me when she didn't think anyone else was around."

Dominic frowned. He was no big fan of Ms. Lakes but this was news to him. "What kind of shots?"

"She'd just tell me how lucky I was to live in a place like the Holden Estate and she often pointed out how I didn't fit in. She'd always made it seem like no one really wanted me to be around and that I was a burden."

"Did you ever tell my grandfather? I'm sure he would have addressed it if you did."

"I was a kid and she was an adult. I didn't think anyone would believe me. So it doesn't matter. I'm still surprised she was let go. She seemed to run the house pretty efficiently even if she was often unpleasant to be around."

"Apparently, she wasn't unpleasant around my grandfather. I think she got it in her head that he needed another 'Mrs.', instead of an estate manager. From my understanding, she became quite aggressive. My grandfather found her naked in his bed." Dominic stopped himself from shuddering with disgust. Some people might have considered the older woman attractive but to him, she'd been a bag of bones with a highly inflated opinion of herself. He wasn't sad to see her go either. Poppy and Felix hadn't cared for her either.

"Wow. She always did seem overly friendly with Uncle Charles."

"Yes, I noticed it but didn't really think about it because even if she tried something it wouldn't have worked. My grandfather had already lost the woman he loved and I'm not sure if he wanted to be with anyone else."

"Your grandmother must have been special."

"She was but that's not who I was talking about." He could have bit his own tongue out for letting that tidbit slip. He hadn't meant to tell her that.

"Who was it?"

"It doesn't matter!" he snapped. When he realized how harsh he sounded, he quickly apologized. "It's been a long night."

She nodded. "Well, as far as Ms. Lakes is concerned, Uncle Charles never seemed to mind when she was being touchy feely with him."

"That's because my grandfather is a nice man. Sometimes too nice."

She grimaced. "Because he took me in?"

He shook his head. "No, actually I wasn't thinking negatively about you."

"At least that time you weren't."

He let out an exasperated sigh. "Krystina, I'm really trying here."

"Sorry."

"It's okay. I wasn't always kind to you."

"No, you weren't."

He sighed. Guilt was starting to get to him but he wouldn't let it. If he started to let it take over him, he'd be forced to reassess everything he believed. He stirred the conversation back to a neutral topic. "Look, I didn't get a chance to tell you because you came straight to your room after business concluded, but I got a call from Sandoval shortly after I arrived back at the suite. He's been called away on an emergency but he should be returning in a couple days to resume business negotiations. So that basically gives us a reprieve. Maybe, we can go do a little touring of the city."

She raised her brows. "Really?"

"Why do you seem so surprised? I'm not that uncultured."

"Roaming the city like a tourist doesn't exactly seem to be your thing. And let's face it, it seems the only time you want to be around me is when you want to..." She cut her gaze away from his.

"I'm not going to lie, duchess. I still want you and we're going to fuck again. But it doesn't mean we can't try to get along for the remainder of the trip. How about we call a truce, at least until we get home?"

It seemed like Krystina was in deep contemplation before she responded. "Okay. You got a deal."

"Good. We'll have an early breakfast and then get a car to see the city. And be sure to pack a bikini."

"Will do."

He caught her chin between his finger and forefinger. "Are you feeling better?"

"Yes. Thanks for checking in on me."

"Anytime." He leaned forward and kissed her on the forehead before leaving the room.

He didn't know what had just happened between them but he felt that something had changed and he wasn't sure if he liked it or not. For so long, he'd had this perception of Krystina because she looked so much like the person who had destroyed his life. He, in turn, had wanted to destroy her.

When he returned to his room and laid down, he looked to the ceiling and whispered, "Mom, what do I do?"

Chapter Fifteen

When Krystina woke up the next morning, she wondered if she'd dreamed the whole thing last night. Dominic had actually been kind to her. It was a side of him that she'd never seen, well at least he'd never shown it to her. She'd witnessed him being affectionate with his brother, sister and Uncle Charles, but she had always been treated as the enemy. It was hard to believe that after all this time, they'd finally had a breakthrough in their relationship. But the problem now was if she was sexually attracted to Dominic when they were enemies, how would she handle being around him when they weren't.

It made her nervous because she wasn't counting on falling for anyone for a while, especially not him. She still had so much of her life to live before she thought about settling down with just one person. "Stop it, Krystina," she muttered to herself. Just because they'd had sex a few times didn't mean it would turn into anything serious. Dominic had always had a different woman on his arm as long as she could remember. She was certain he would eventually move on from her. And she was fine with that eventuality.

She had to be.

After a long shower, she put on a white strapless bikini and white mini sundress. She took care to slather sunscreen over her dark skin for protection under the punishing Spanish sun. She braided her hair in a French braid and decided to go without makeup.

She was actually excited about seeing the sites because she would get to take pictures. She took out the professional grade camera from her bag and made it photo ready.

There was another impressive spread on the table but Dominic wasn't there. A note addressed to her rested on the table. With a frown, she picked it up and read.

Went for a run on the beach. When I get back and shower, we can go sightseeing. Help yourself to breakfast. Dominic.

Krystina didn't know if she was disappointed or relieved that he wasn't at the table, but him being gone gave her the opportunity to eat in peace and mentally plan the things she wanted to do today. She scrolled through her phone and looked at potential spots to visit. By the time she finished breakfast, a shirtless Dominic returned. He was wearing a pair of athletic shorts and running shoes. An MP3 was tethered to a band around his arm. His hair was wet and his body glistened with sweat. Krystina's mouth went dry at the sight of unadulterated masculinity. Visions of their bodies sliding together entered her head and she immediately rid herself of those images. This man had cast some kind of spell on her because why else would she suddenly react this way whenever he walked into a room.

"Good, you're up. I trust you had a good night's sleep after I left your room?"

She could only nod, not trusting herself to speak.

"Well, I'm going to hop in the shower now. I'll be ready to go when I'm done."

"Uh, aren't you going to eat something?"

"I had some coffee and some eggs before my run. I'll probably grab a banana before we leave." He smiled at her and she believed it was actually the first genuine smile she'd ever received from it. It had a devastating effect. It was going to be a long day.

Later that day, as they were driving along the coast, Krystina snapped pictures. She snapped shots of everything from the people to food to landmarks and anything of interest. She was happiest with her camera in hand.

"You think you've taken enough pictures?" Dominic asked from the driver's seat?

"Never. As long as I have film, there's always time for one more shot."

"I didn't realize you enjoyed photography so much. I had noticed your equipment earlier but I thought you are one of those people with fancy equipment who don't know how to use it."

"Oh, I definitely know how to use it and I'm quite good at it," she said without conceit. One of her favorite things about discovering a new place was taking pictures of them to always have the memory preserved.

"I didn't realize you were such a Jill of all trades. You're great at languages and you're an ace photographer. What made you decide to choose a job as a translator instead of going into photography?"

"It was a more practical choice. With the way the world is changing, it's handy to know several languages, especially in the field of international business. Photography isn't as easy to break into. The kind of pictures I'd like to take for a living are the kind you'd see in nature and travel magazines."

"No screaming babies in studios?"

"I wouldn't mind taking pictures of babies but the types of baby pictures people carry around in their wallets aren't my thing."

"Why is that?"

"They're so staged. I like capturing things in their most natural state. The best pictures of people are when they're unaware of when they're being captured on film. That's when you see the real essence of a person. Like now." She raised her camera and snapped a picture of Dominic's profile.

"I hate having my picture taken."

"Why is that?"

"Because they lie."

"Pictures don't lie. They tell a story, it's up to the viewer to interpret what that tale actually is."

"When I was younger, my mother used to make a big deal about taking family pictures. She'd insisted that we have them taken for each holiday and we'd smile for the camera presenting this picture of the big happy family when we were anything but. It was all a big lie. After my mother died, I never sat down for another photo."

Dominic had never mentioned his mother before, but then again, the two of them had never been much for talking to the other. This was the most honest conversation they'd ever had.

"I'm sorry to hear that. Were you and your parents close?"

"I'd rather not talk about this with you."

She stiffened. He didn't say he didn't want to talk about it, just that he didn't want to talk about it with her. It was clear there were still certain boundaries between them that she wasn't allowed to cross. Deciding it was best to keep quiet, she resumed taking pictures.

They drove in silence for several more minutes before Dominic turned down a private stretch of road. "Where are we going?"

"A buddy of mine owns property here. He has a private beach. I figured it would be better to go here instead of battling for a good spot with a bunch of tourists."

"Will your friend mind that we're here?"

"Not at all. He said that I can use this place whenever I was in the area."

"Must be nice," she muttered. Somehow the magic of the day was lost and she wasn't sure how they could get it back.

As it turned out, Dominic's friend wasn't in residence but Dominic knew the codes to get in.

"Why don't you go change into your bathing suit? And then we'll head outside to the beach. There are some lounge chairs out there. I'll go get us some towels and bottled water."

Krystina merely nodded. The only thing she had to do was slip off her dress. She put on a big floppy hat and a pair of sunglasses. Not wanting to wait for Dominic, she headed outside without him. The sight that greeted her was breathtaking. Pulling her camera out again, she took some photos of the picturesque scenery. Once she's taken enough. She found a lounge chair and adjusted it so that she could lay down. She loved the feel of the sun against her bare skin. She lay on her stomach soaking up the rays. She must have drifted off because she woke up to something cold on her back.

She jerked away from the hand moving up and down her back. Turning her head, her gaze collided with Dominic's.

"What are you doing?" she said drowsily.

"I'm putting sunscreen on your back. You don't want to burn do you?"

"Thank you." She whispered.

Dominic kneaded the lotion into her skin. Before she realized what he was doing, he unhooked the back of her bikini and was caressing her skin. She didn't know whether he was applying lotion or using this as a prelude to something more.

When his hand went lower, slipping on the inside of her bikini bottom she had her answer.

"Dominic," she began.

"Shh. You had to know what would happen when I saw you in this tiny excuse for a swimsuit. You're practically begging to be fucked and I'm more than willing to oblige."

She whimpered when he pulled down her bottoms and tossed them aside. Krystina remained on her stomach, scared to show how eager she was for his touch. This mercurial relationship they had was so confusing. One second they were barely talking and then the next, they couldn't keep their hands off of each other. She was certain that by the time they went home, she'd be an emotional wreck.

He trailed his finger down the center of her crack before sliding it across her pussy lips. "Already wet for me. Tell me what you're thinking, duchess."

"I'm thinking that you're confusing me."

"Oh? How so?"

"We seemed to be having a good day and having a good conversation, but then you shut me out. You go from hot to cold within the blink of an eye and I don't know how to react around you."

He didn't answer. Instead, he started to rub her pussy, drawing a gasp from her lips. He nudged her legs apart. "It's been nearly twenty-four hours since I was inside this pussy." He slipped two fingers inside her channel shoved them deep within her.

She noticed that he'd didn't respond to what she'd said, but at this point, it really didn't matter because once again, her body had completely given in to is touch.

"Dominic, what are you doing to me?" Krystina moaned.

"Making you feel good. But, I think it's time for you to return the favor." He whispered against her ear as he pumped his fingers in and out of her hot hole.

"What?" She asked breathlessly.

"Turn over and see for yourself." He pulled his fingers out of her, allowing Krystina more movement.

She rolled to her back to see he'd kicked off his swim trucks and he stood in all his nude glory. He was like a Greek God, so beautifully toned and unashamed. His hard cock jutted forward. "He wants a kiss," Dominic said, indicating his dick.

Krystina had wanted to take him into her mouth since their first time but she hadn't been bold enough to go for it. Throwing caution to the wind, she slid off the lounger and dropped to her knees. She tilted her head back as she circled his cock with her fingers so that she could gauge his reaction.

"Do it," he groaned. "Take me in your mouth."

Leaning forward she ran her tongue around his velvety-textured head before pulling him into her mouth. She bobbed her head forward taking him in a little at a time until her she couldn't fit any more in. She moved her lips back and forth, wetting his hard shaft with saliva. Krystina gripped the base of his shaft in her fist and continued to suck him in earnest. With her free hand, she cradled his balls and gave them a slight squeeze.

He inhaled sharply. "Oh yeah, duchess, just like that. Your mouth feels amazing."

Krystina ran her tongue along his length, reveling in the taste of him on her tongue. A pearl-like drop of his cum sat at the tip of his cock which she flicked with her tongue before taking him in her mouth again. He was so thick she couldn't fit all of him in, but she tried until the tip hit the back of her throat.

He gripped the sides of her head and growled. "Oh shit! Where the fuck did you learn to do that?"

Dominic gyrated his hips moving in tandem with Krystina. He stiffened. "I'm going to come." He attempted to pull away from her, but she grabbed him by his hips to anchor him to her.

"Fuck!" He yelled.

Warm salty cream filled her mouth when he thrust forward. Krystina attempted to catch all she could, but some of his seed dribbled down her chin. Only when she was certain he was finished did she pull back. With a grin, she looked up at him and wiped the sides of her mouth.

For once Dominic appeared to be rendered speechless and it gave Krystina a sense of power that she could have such a strong effect on this sexy man. "Did you like it?" She asked already knowing the answer to the question.

Still, no words came from his mouth. Emboldened by this sexual awakening within her, Krystina stood and begin to kiss Dominic along his jaw line. She stood on the tip of her toes and nipped his earlobe with her teeth making him groan.

She ran her fingertips along the hard plane of his chest to feel his taut muscles beneath her fingers. His breathing became shallow. She'd always allowed her lovers to take the lead but there was something liberating about being the aggressor. Krystina circled his nipple with her fingertip before flicking it with her tongue.

Dominic moaned. "What are you doing to me woman?"

"Making you feel good," she answered before turning her attention to his other nipple. Running her hand down the length of his body she encountered his cock which sprang to attention again.

"I know a way you can make me feel really good."

She raised a brow in question. "Show me."

Dominic took her hand and led her back to the lounger. He adjusted the apparatus enough so that he was leaning back when he took a seat on it. "I want you to ride me."

She moistened her lips, eyeing his erection. This was another first for her, but she was so hot right now, Dominic could have suggested any sexual position at this point and she would have been game.

Krystina swung her leg over the chair and straddled him before slowly lowering herself until her pussy hovered over his cock.

"Guide it inside of you, duchess. You're in control right now."

She began to shake in anticipation as she took his dick in her hand and aligned it with her entrance. Already wet and ready for his invasion, she had no problem fully seating herself on his cock.

"Aww, yeah, that's it, duchess. You have the most addictive pussy."

Krystina gripped his shoulders and raised herself just a bit before plopping back down on him. It took her a few moments to find her rhythm but when she finally did, she couldn't stop.

In this position, his dick was so deep inside of her, she didn't know where she ended and he began. They were like one unit, moving together in sexual harmony. Dominic dug his fingers into her hips creating the most delicious pleasure. She could barely stand it.

As she continued to bounce on his dick, her body become inflamed with desire.

"Lean forward," he said in between breaths. "I want to suck on those beautiful brown babies."

Doing as he commanded, Krystina cried out when he leaned forward and captured one nipple in his mouth. He nibbled on it none to gently but she loved every moment of it. The muscles in her thighs strained from exertion but she couldn't stop. She was hurtling toward a peak so explosive nothing could have prevented it.

So when her orgasm hit her, Krystina nearly blacked out from pleasure overload. Dominic took over, raising his hips and thrusting from below until he released a primal cry. She felt his warm seed shot inside of her.

Unable to hold herself stable any longer, she collapsed against his hard frame. Dominic wrapped his arms around her. "That was amazing, duchess." He kissed the top of her head.

She was too breathless to respond. If the rest of her trip went like this, she'd go home a very sore woman.

Chapter Sixteen

Dominic signed the documents in front of him and then put them in the bag for the courier to send to his lawyers. These were the papers that would make his partnership with the Sandoval Group official. Though the trip had been a month ago, there had still been some minor details to iron out. All in all, it had been a successful trip. Both companies were able to get something they wanted. Holden's would have access to parts of the island that they didn't have before and Sandoval's would be able to include Holden's as a part of their tour packages for a deep discount. It was a deal that would make both parties a lot of money in the future.

Business aside, something had changed between him and Krystina. When they weren't in business meetings with Sandoval and his employees, they were exploring the island together. Surprisingly, Krystina was a great travel partner because she was well-versed in the culture of the people and because she'd researched the island beforehand. Her face seemed to light up whenever she discovered something new and she was actually quite funny. He would never have guessed that she had a great sense of humor. He found himself actually enjoying her company. And at night, they fucked like rabbits but the problem with that was, he wasn't exactly sure that it was fucking anymore. It was something else. Something he couldn't put into words and he wasn't exactly sure how to feel about it.

For so long, he'd felt nothing but animosity toward her because of who she was and what she represented to him but the week in Ibiza with her made him realize that maybe he'd been wrong the entire time. She was just a kid, after all, perhaps he didn't give her a fair shake.

Their last night in Spain kept playing in his mind.

He collapsed on top of Krystina once he'd spilled all his essence. No matter how many times they had sex, he couldn't seem to get enough of her. Dominic thought he'd be able to get her out of his system with a few quick fucks, but the more they did it, the more he wanted her. He wondered if it was true what his grandfather had said about the Jackson women. If it was, he didn't want to be a victim of whatever kind of spell she might place on him.

He should have rolled off the bed and told her to go back to her room while he showered to wash the scent of her off of him, but he couldn't bring himself to do that. He liked the feel of her in his arms. Dominic enjoyed the soft touch of her hand resting on his chest. He liked the comfortable silence that fell between them in the afterglow of what they'd done.

Krystina raised her head to look at him. "Dominic?"

"Hmm?"

"We're going home tomorrow."

"I know."

"This trip...it was...nice."

"Yeah."

"When we go back, I don't want things to be the way they used to be. With us, constantly at each other's throat. I don't know what this thing is that we have, but I just know that I don't want to fight with you anymore."

Dominic didn't answer at first. In truth, he didn't want to fight anymore either but it was hard letting go of an anger he'd held on to for so long. He still had the nightmares about the night that changed his life. How could he let that go? But then again, he was so tired of the back and forth. And it would probably make his grandfather happy to see the two of them getting along. "I think we can manage that. I know I haven't always been the kindest person but I think we can manage to get along." He didn't bother to mention the fact that he had no intention to stop having sex with her, but he thought that went without saying.

There had been a vulnerability in Krystina's voice when she'd made that plea to him and he couldn't ignore it. So far since the trip, not only had they managed to get along, they actually had conversations that weren't centered around work. Krystina had even taken him to the makeshift darkroom that she made in a utility closet in the basement to develop her pictures. Dominic didn't know a lot about photography, but he wasn't so ignorant as not to realize that she was extremely talented. She seemed to capture the very essence of people on film. There had been pictures of landscapes and of children and some of the hotel. Her photos seemed to tell a story. She was a woman of hidden depths. If circumstances were different, he might actually allow himself to fall for her, but he couldn't allow himself that last betrayal.

The phone on his desk rung and he saw that the light indicated that it was an inside call. "Yes, Eileen," he answered.

"I was just calling to let you know I'll be heading out to lunch. But, Ms. Jackson would like to see you. Is it okay to send her in?"

"Yes. Go ahead."

Krystina had been out of the office the past few days because she'd gone on a trip to Beijing with a couple of the directors. Dominic couldn't go because he had to visit the Vegas location because part of the building had caught on fire. He thought the time apart might have been good for them, but all he could do on his trip was think about her.

There was a light tap on his door.

"Come in."

Krystina walked into his office with two white paper bags in hand. "Good afternoon."

He gave her a slight smile. "I didn't think you'd be in the office today. What time did your flight get in?"

"This morning."

"And you decided to come to work today. You could have taken the day off to recover. It's Friday, after all."

"It's okay. I like keeping busy. Besides, John Norbert wanted me to translate some documents for him and I wanted to start working on them."

"What do you have there?" He eyed the bags in her hand.

"Lunch. I know you haven't had any and I picked some up on the way in."

This revelation took him by surprise. A couple months ago if anyone would have told him that Krystina would actually be seeking him out and buying him lunch, he would have laughed in their faces. The dynamics between them had certainly changed but he'd think about them later. Right now, he was actually hungry. "Whatcha got for me?"

"I bought paninis from the deli down the street with extra oil and vinegar."

"The caprese chicken paninis?" He perked up at the sound of one of his favorite sandwiches.

"Yep. When we had the staff meeting and ordered lunch, I remembered you favoring them."

"Thanks. That's very nice of you for remembering that." He took the bag from her feeling slightly guilty. "So, how was your trip?"

"It went smoothly. Not everyone in the Zhang group spoke English so my skills came in handy. They had their own interpreter, though. He was very thorough in getting our groups point across. I'm sure you'll get a full report from John and Peter when you meet up with them."

He nodded. "Glad to hear it." He took a bite of his sandwich.

"How did it go in Vegas?"

"Things went well. The fire didn't damage nearly as much as I originally thought and what it did destroy, the insurance will take care of it. We'll have to close off that part of the resort while it's being renovated."

"And how long will it take to get it back into working conditions?" Krystina nibbled on her panini.

"A few months."

"How will that affect profits?"

"Some of the amenities won't be available for guests so we'll probably have to offer deep discounts in the meantime."

"That might not be a bad thing. I mean if you have to temporarily discount rates that might bring in some new people who weren't able to afford a stay there. Possibly people who are having bachelor or bachelorette parties who want to do it up or just people who want to go to Vegas and luxuriate in all the amenities that Holden's has to offer."

"That's not a bad idea actually. I had given that a thought but I want to stay true to our brand as far as Holden's resorts go. But I have been working on another project to bring a taste of what we have to offer on a smaller more affordable scale. It's currently in the planning stages right now."

"That's great. I'm guessing you'll be pretty busy in the coming months."

He nodded. "I will but I also have a team that will be heading up that endeavor so the work will be pretty evenly distributed."

"That's good."

He raised a brow. "Good?"

"Yes. You work too much. You should take time to relax sometimes."

Dominic chuckled. "Careful Krystina, if you keep this up, I might actually think you care."

She fell silent and took a bite of her sandwich instead of responding to him right away. When she did, her words took him by surprise. "Maybe, I do."

Dominic threw his head back and laughed out loud. "I think the only thing you really care about is my dick. But don't worry, duchess, you don't have to bribe me with lunch to get it."

Krystina who had been in the process of taking another bite of her sandwich froze. "Excuse me?"

"You heard me. You've been away for a few days. Don't fool yourself into thinking this is about me. You're just addicted to the sex. Just like I am."

"I see." She stood up abruptly. "Well, thank you for letting me know how *I* feel. Like I said before, I have some documents I need to look through. I'll let you get back to whatever you were doing before I interrupted you." She turned around and left his office.

When Krystina was gone, he exhaled and sunk into his chair. What he'd said was a bit crass but it was the truth. The only thing that there was between them right now was the sex. Sure it helped matters that they were cordial with each other because of their intimate relationship, but she didn't have to pretend they were more than what they were. Fuckbuddies.

It might have been harsh, but this was the way it had to be. Dominic was beginning to feel things that were better left alone and he just couldn't risk letting down someone whose memory he vowed to preserve.

With a sigh, he opened his desk and pulled out the framed picture of his mother. She's been a beauty with long blonde hair and aqua eyes. She wore her signature smile. He remembered that she used to smile a lot until things fell apart. And then, the only time he saw her smile after that was when he looked into the family portraits.

This was a picture that was taken when Dominic was younger during a time when he thought he belonged to a happy family, but it had all been a façade. He remembered Krystina's words about photographs not lying which made him take a closer look and he noticed something that he hadn't before. The smile that he once thought was a happy one seemed strained and there were shadows under her eyes that makeup couldn't quite cover. If he inspected it even more closely, he could see tiny frown lines etching the corners of her mouth.

The truth had been in this picture all along and he'd never noticed it. Seeing this gave him the reason to remain firm in his resolve. He touched the glass that protected his mother's face with his fingertips. "I won't let you, down," he whispered.

Krystina felt like an idiot. What did she think she'd get out of being friendly with Dominic? She was foolish to believe that he wanted to change and it was even sillier of her to believe that something could come out of their erotic encounters. In the beginning, she couldn't figure out what it was about Dominic that made her give in to him so easily. Sure he was an expert lover who could draw things out of her that no other man could, but it was more than that. It was more than that and the second she realized what it was, it frightened the hell out of her.

She had fallen in love with Dominic.

It was an insane concept considering how badly he'd treated her over the years and she'd tried to analyze what the hell was wrong with her. But the more she thought about it, the more it made her realize that she'd never really hated him. Whenever he had lashed out at her, she'd given it back as a defense mechanism, but deep down, she was just a lost little girl looking for approval. There were times he'd actually be decent toward her and she lapped up the attention. But then he'd return to form and fall back into the role of her tormentor.

Despite it all, deep down there was a spark of hope within her that they could one day get along and be friends. But somewhere along the way, this hope for them to be friends became something more. It was around the time she started college and she'd come home from break. Up until then, she'd grown quite used to Dominic dating lots of different women. Some had even come around the house, but there was one in particular that simply got under her skin.

Her name was Veronica Mathers who was a self-proclaimed model. It was clear, Veronica wasn't the high-end fashion model. She was the type who had been in a few department store catalogs and constantly put pictures of herself on social media and called herself a model. In Krystina's mind, the woman was just waiting around for a rich husband to take care of her, because the only thing she had to rely on were her looks. Having a conversation with the woman was like talking to a sack of rocks even though Krystina was certain the rocks were smarter.

Veronica had stuck around the longest and Krystina found herself getting agitated whenever the other woman was around. And when she'd walked into a room to find Dominic and Veronica kissing, Krystina had wanted to be sick. She told herself that what Dominic did had no bearing on her because she hated him, but that wasn't true. At the realization of why Veronica bothered her, Krystina avoided Dominic as much as she could.

And then, the kiss happened.

When Dominic had kissed her, it was like he'd found out the truth and was mocking her. He was throwing her feelings back in her face and at that point, she really did hate him. It was why she'd left the country. She couldn't be around him because it hurt too much. She never thought when she came home that he would pursue her in the way he had. And when she was in his arms, she never questioned why. That trip to Ibiza had changed something between them. Sometimes when they were together, they'd be frantic for one other and other times, he'd take her so sweetly she wanted to cry. It was like she was dealing with two different Dominics.

And now they had some kind sexual exchange happening between them, and she'd caught feelings, which is what she'd been scared of all along. After what he'd said to her in the office, it was clear that he didn't feel the same way and probably never would. For her own sanity, she had to figure out a way to break this chain of control he seemed to have on her soul before he completely consumed it.

By the time she made it home, she was exhausted. The house was quiet because Felix and Poppy were back in school and Uncle Charles mainly stayed in the west wing where his bedroom and sitting rooms were when he wasn't at his private gentlemen's club.

When she walked by the family room, she was surprised to see lights on and hear voices. She walked into the room and saw Uncle Charles and Mr. Shaw, his longtime friend in a deep discussion. Uncle Charles was the first to notice her.

The older man smiled. "Krystina, my dear. Come on in. I take it that you and Dominic didn't ride home together."

She shook her head. "We don't go to work together because our schedules are a bit different. Besides, I just came in from Beijing earlier and went into the office later."

"That's right. This old man brain of mine tends to forget at times. You remember my old friend, Cooper Shaw, don't you?"

Krystina nodded and smiled. "Hello, Mr. Shaw."

The other man smiled back. "It's nice to see you again, Krystina. Charles was just telling me how well traveled you are and that you're quite a whiz with languages."

"It's just something I have a knack for. It's no big deal."

"Oh, it's a very big deal. And if you're ever looking for a job, we can always use your sort of talent."

Uncle Charles shook his head with a chuckle. "She works for Holden's. Don't think you can just snatch her from us."

"Well, the young lady could change her mind and if she does she should give me a call. Krystina, do you remember my nephew, Tyler?"

She smiled politely. "Of course." She hadn't seen Tyler since that embarrassing incident when Dominic had caught them making out. They'd emailed and texted each other afterward but soon communication dwindled until it became non-existent. She had always meant to inquire about him but never had the opportunity.

Mr. Shaw grinned. "Well, he certainly remembers you. When I told him you were back home, he was eager to come over."

She tilted her head to the side. "He's here?"

"Yes. He's in the bathroom and should be out shortly."

Before she could respond, someone called out her name. "Krystina!"
She turned around and saw a tall blond who looked as if he stepped off the cover of a men's magazine. "Tyler?"
She raced into his open arms and gave him a huge hug.

Chapter Seventeen

"Oh my God, you didn't!" Krystina let out a combination of a scream and laugh. Her sides actually hurt from laughing so hard.

"It's true. I can't believe all the dumbass things I did pledging to that fraternity. I'm surprised I made it through school alive."

Tyler had spent the last half hour regaling her about all of his college antics. Krystina couldn't remember laughing like this in a long time. After seeing Tyler, he suggested that the two of them go out to dinner to catch up on old times. Uncle Charles and Mr. Shaw said they'd be okay by themselves and that the cook would take care of their meals.

After her stressful encounter with Dominic, Krystina was happy for this reprieve. It was as if no time had passed since they'd last seen each other. She felt so relaxed and comfortable around Tyler. They decided to go to a Brazilian Steak House that she'd always wanted to try. The food had been excellent but the company was even better. She'd been reluctant for the evening to end once dinner was over, so Tyler suggested they go back to his place.

Krystina had been surprised when she discovered that Tyler was only a half an hour away from the mansion and he explained that he's recently moved closer to his Uncle to start working in his company. It was good to know she had a friend so close by.

Now they sat in the middle of his living room floor, eating ice cream and catching up. She didn't realize how much she'd needed this until now. "Well, we all did some crazy things when we were younger."

"Not you, from what I understand, you studied abroad and then went traveling the world. My Uncle told me that you even did some volunteer work. That's pretty darn amazing." His eyes gleamed with admiration making her blush.

"It's just something I wanted to do. When I was younger, I didn't grow up with much. Me and my grandmother lived in this little two bedroom house with the barest amenities and none of the luxuries that kids are used to today. But, we made do. I didn't realize we were poor until Uncle Charles took us in and I knew then that I always wanted to give back to society in some way."

"That's pretty amazing, Krystina. I know this is going to make me sound like a total creeper but I'd kept up with you on social media. I saw some of the pictures you posted and was so proud of you."

Tyler's confession surprised her. She'd thought about him over the years, occasionally. She thought he'd forgotten all about her. "Why didn't you ever send me a friend request? It would have been great to hear from you."

"Because, I felt guilty. You and I were good friends and then when I finally told you how I felt, it turned into a big old mess."

Krystina rolled her eyes. "Because Dominic messed things up."

"Yeah, but I was so embarrassed that I was afraid that you'd laugh at me when you saw me again."

"I never would have laughed at you, Tyler. Dominic was being a dick, I know it wasn't your fault."

"I always wondered what would have happened if we would have progressed beyond that. If you and I could have made it as a couple."

She moistened her suddenly dry lips. Krystina had often wondered the answer to that question too. "Me, too."

"Krystina, you can say no if you'd like but I was wondering…can I kiss you?"

She wasn't sure if she wanted to complicate matters when they'd just reconnected so soon. But on the other hand, it wasn't as if she owed Dominic anything. He'd made it quite clear to her that she meant nothing to him beyond being a piece of ass. Why the hell not? At least, if she let Tyler kiss her, she wouldn't have to always wonder about what if.

"Yes," she whispered leaning forward to meet his lips.

He cupped the back of her head in his palm as he pressed his mouth against hers. The first thing she noted was that Tyler's lips were nice and soft but they weren't as full as Dominic's. She quickly shoved all thought of him out of her mind and focused on the kiss. Tyler pressed his tongue against her lips seeking entrance and she parted her lips. He moved closer pulled her against him. Krystina returned his kiss with as much enthusiasm as she could muster. When Tyler touched her breast, it felt good but she didn't burst into flames like she expected she would.

Their tongues danced entwining and licking each other, and all the while Krystina couldn't help but think something was off. It wasn't like she wasn't enjoying it,

Tyler was actually quite a good kisser but she had expected more.

Finally, he pulled away with an expectant smile. "What did you think?"

She placed her hand on the side of his face. "I think that was very nice, Tyler."

"There's a 'but' in there somewhere, isn't there?"

She sighed. "Don't get me wrong, I did like it but it's...I can't really explain it. Tyler now that we've reconnected, I don't want to lose you again. You were one of my best friends."

"Ah, the old, it's me not you line." It hurt her to see that she'd hurt him. This wasn't how she wanted to end her night.

Krystina took his hand in hers. "Please don't take it that way. I'd really like for us to be friends again. And I'm sure, there are plenty women who would line up to be with you." Tyler was a very good looking man. She was surprised to learn that he was single.

"Tyler, you can't tell me that you're not beating women off with a stick."

"Well, I've had some serious girlfriends over the years, but I guess you'll always be the one who got away."

"Or, I could be the one who becomes a really great friend."

He didn't say anything at first as if he were weighing his options. Finally, he smiled. "Yeah, you're right. I'd really like that, Krystina."

She gave him a hug, happy they'd reached an understanding. Krystina eyed the clock on the wall and saw that it was well nearly one in the morning. "Oh, God, I should probably get home."

"You don't have to rush off. Tomorrow is Saturday. I have a spare bedroom and an extra toothbrush."

Krystina really didn't want to go home and chance a run in with Dominic. The idea of staying away for a night sounded more appealing by the second. "You know, I think I'll take you up on that offer."

Dominic paced the kitchen floor trying to burn off some nervous energy. He'd already run for an hour on the treadmill and he still hadn't calmed down. He could feel the vein throbbing in his head and the rage that flared within his chest made it nearly impossible to breathe.

After a stressful day in the office, he'd thought about not coming home because he didn't want to face Krystina. The hurt in her eyes that he'd spied earlier was something he couldn't stop thinking about. He wanted to give her a proper apology and finally, explain to her why he had to keep her at arms length emotionally. He thought she at least deserved that.

But when he came home, it was to find his Grandfather and his good friend, Cooper Shaw.

It was well past dinnertime by the time he arrived home. His grandfather was probably already in his private sitting room enjoying a glass of bourbon and watching an old movie which is what he liked to do before going to bed. He was surprised, however, to hear laughter coming from the living room. His grandfather was smoking a cigar while listening to his old friend, Cooper Shaw.

"Good evening."

"Dominic, my boy. Didn't think you'd put in an appearance tonight. You missed a very nice dinner. The cook

made the most fantastic roast. Come join us. We'd love the company." *His grandfather waved him over.*

"Hello, Mr. Shaw."

"Oh, you don't have to be so formal with me. You're a man. Call me, Cooper."

Dominic smiled politely before taking a seat in a nearby armchair.

"So your grandfather told me that you were doing a stellar job running Holden's. I'm glad that he has someone competent to take over the reins."

"Thank you."

"Yes, I couldn't be prouder of him." *His grandfather smiled.* "I'd always hoped that his father would be running things one day with Dominic as his heir, but Henry never really had much of a head for business."

Dominic was surprised that his grandfather had mentioned his father so freely. From what Dominic could tell, father and son hadn't seen eye to eye on many issues but he knew for a fact that his grandfather had taken his son's death to heart. Grandfather rarely talked about his son and when he did it was always with a heaviness.

"I know what you mean, Charles. None of my daughters were interested in going into business but thank goodness for Tyler. I think he'll do well. He's already showing an aptitude for the job. He'll be taking the lead in no time."

Dominic had only been half listening when he heard the name, Tyler. He'd forgotten that Cooper Shaw's nephew was the same punk who used to sniff around Krystina.

"He's become a fine young man. So glad he and Krystina could reconnect. Those two used to be joined at the hip when they were younger. I don't know what happened," *Grandfather wondered aloud.*

Cooper shrugged. "People drift apart but I'm sure they'll do plenty of catching up tonight."

Dominic sat on the edge of his seat. "What do you mean?"

His grandfather smiled. "They went out for dinner."

"And they're not back, yet?"

Grandfather frowned. "It's only nine-thirty. I'm sure they're fine."

Dominic had zoned out after that. After an acceptable amount of time to excuse himself passed, he did exactly that.

It was three in the morning and Krystina had yet to come home. He couldn't stop thinking about what she was doing with that boy. Was she giving that bastard the sweet pussy that belonged exclusively to him? He swore when he saw Krystina, he'd fuck her so hard, she wouldn't be able to look at another man without thinking of him.

"Dominic, what are you doing up so late? I would think you'd be in bed by now." He turned to see his grandfather walking into the kitchen.

"I could ask the same thing of you."

"My arthritis is acting up. I couldn't sleep so I thought I'd fix myself some warm milk."

Dominic smirked. His grandfather's idea of warm milk was forty percent milk and sixty percent whiskey. That would knock anyone out. "Take it easy with that stuff, okay?"

"Boy, I've been fixing these concoctions before you were a twitch in your father's pants. I'll take it easy when I'm dead. So back to my original question, what are you doing pacing the kitchen floor so late at night," his grandfather asked as he gathered the ingredients to make his drink.

"Just thinking about work."

Charles stood in mid-action. "Don't lie to me, Dominic."

His grandfather always seemed to know when he wasn't telling the truth. Because of that, Dominic didn't bother to lie to him until now. He sighed. "Krystina isn't home yet."

The older man gave him a long penetrating stare before resuming his activity. "She's twenty-three years old and an adult by everyone's standards. Just as you're allowed to come and go as you please, so is she."

"But what decent girl, stays out this late with some guy she hasn't seen in years."

Grandfather put his beverage in the microwave and pressed the button to turn it on. "I'm going to pretend you didn't say that."

Dominic ran his finger through his hair in frustration. "I didn't mean for it to come out that way."

"You know, Dominic, you've always been more of a son to me than your father. Because of what you've gone through, I've always given you more leeway than I should have. I wish I would have said something to you years ago but I feared I'd drive you away like I did your father, but I'm going to say it now because you need to hear it. Krystina is not Candice. She's not Willie Mae. Your father and I made the mistakes that we did and went about things the wrong way, but that doesn't mean you have to as well. What happened in the past, is in the past."

"I don't know what you're talking about."

"Yes, the hell you do. Straighten your ass up right now or you're going to lose her. You don't think I see the way you look at her when you're in a room together. How you've looked at her since she was sixteen years old."

Dominic shook his head in denial. "You must be mistaken."

"I may be old, but I'm not blind. Like I said before, it's time to say the things to you that I should have said a long time ago. I know she went abroad because something happened between the two of you. I don't know for sure, but I had a hunch. How you used to treat her was inexcusable. I didn't want to play favorites so while I didn't speak to you about your treatment of her, I shielded her the best that I could. That's why I spoiled Krystina and tried to make her feel as much a part of the family as the rest of you. But, something has changed and it's got you pacing the kitchen floor at three in the morning because you're jealous she's having a night out with a friend. There's a crack in this foundation, Dominic, and you better fix it before it's broken beyond repair."

And with that, his grandfather took his drink and left Dominic standing in the middle of the kitchen.

Chapter Eighteen

Krystina woke up to the smell of bacon and coffee. She stretched beneath the comfy blanket and opened her eyes. This wasn't her bed. She sat up and looked around her. It took a few moments before the events of the previous night returned to her. She and Tyler had hung out until the wee hours in the morning stuffing their faces with junk food and watching bad B movies like they were teenagers again.

She felt bad that she couldn't return his romantic interest in her but he seemed to take it in stride. He didn't bring it up again or try anything for the rest of the night. She slid out of bed and shivered. All she was wearing was one of the oversized t-shirts that Tyler had let her borrow.

She left the bedroom and followed the scent of the food. Tyler was making eggs on the stove. "Morning sleepyhead, or should I say, good afternoon?" He greeted without turning away from what he was cooking.

"Afternoon? What time is it?"

"It's almost two o'clock"

"Two? Oh my God, I can't believe I slept that long. I usually don't sleep in like that."

"Well, we didn't go to bed until five in morning with our bellies full of carbs. That combination alone is enough to put the most seasoned insomniac to sleep."

"What time did you wake up?"

"About an hour ago. I showered and dressed and decided to cook us something to eat. I know it's in the afternoon but my first meal has to be breakfast food or my day just doesn't go well."

"I know what you mean. Did I smell coffee? I sure could use a cup."

"Coming right up." He grabbed a mug from one of the cabinets and turned around to hand it to her. Tyler froze as he took in her attire. "Wow, that shirt looks way better on you than it ever did on me."

"Uh, thanks." She shifted on her feet feeling slightly uncomfortable all of a sudden.

He chuckled. "Don't worry about it. I won't try anything. Just admiring the view."

"You don't have a robe I could borrow, do you? It's a bit chilly in here."

"Oh sure, let me go grab you one."

While he went to retrieve a robe, she fixed herself a cup of coffee. She sighed with relief when she took the first sip. "Mmm, this is good stuff," Krystina said when Tyler returned to the kitchen. "I haven't had coffee this good since I was in Kenya. Now that country knows how to do coffee."

"You know your coffees because that's exactly what that is. Have a seat and I'll fix a plate for you." Tyler handed her the robe which she gladly took.

Breakfast consisted of bacon, eggs and burnt toast which she teased Tyler mercilessly about. Once they were finished, she helped him wash up. Since she had no plans that day, he suggested they go to the movies. In no rush to go back home, Krystina agreed. They went bowling afterward and then out to dinner. It wasn't until later that night when Krystina decided it was time to go home and only because she didn't feel like wearing the same clothes again.

She left Tyler with the promise of meeting up again soon. It was great to spend a stress-free day without worrying about how Dominic would treat her. Spending time with Tyler, made Krystina realize she deserved so much better than what Dominic had to offer, no matter how Earth shattering the sex was.

The mansion was dark when she walked inside. She hummed to herself as she headed straight to her room. Once she flicked on the light, she let out a startled yelp when she saw Dominic sitting on her bed.

"Dominic, what are you doing here?"

"Obviously, waiting for you."

"Okay," she said as calmly as possible. "Let me rephrase my question. Why are you waiting for me?"

"Isn't it obvious? You didn't come home last night."

"So? In case you've forgotten, I'm off on the weekends. I can do what I want in my free time."

He was off the bed in a shot and before she realized what was happening, he gripped her by the forearm. "And, you seem to have forgotten who this pussy belongs to. Did you spread your legs for him?"

After all, he'd put her through, he had a lot of nerve. She smacked him across the face as hard as she could. Instead of getting him off of her, it seemed to set him off. "So you like to play rough? Okay, we'll do things your way."

Dominic lifted her off her feet but Krystina kicked and clawed at him refusing to give in to him. "Let me go, you asshole!"

"Not a chance. Not until I get what you gave him last night."

"If I did, it's none of your business."

"Oh, but it is." He threw her on the bed and she immediately tried to scramble away from him but to no avail. He gripped her by the ankle and pulled her toward him. He fell on top of her, grabbed her wrists and pinned them above her head. She raised her pelvis to buck him off but he was like a boulder weighing down on her.

He lowered his head toward hers but she turned away from his kiss. Dominic's lips fell on her cheek and then he moved down to her neck and sucked on her vulnerable flesh until she cried out. Krystina didn't want to respond but like always, the second he touched her, she went up into flames. But still, she tried to resist. She vowed not to make this easy for him.

He was able to hold both of her wrists in one hand while he unbuckled her jeans with the other. "Stop this now!"

"Never. You challenged me when you stayed out all night with that boy. So now, it's my turn."

Dominic released her arms long enough to yank her pants down. She kicked him in the stomach making him double over. Krystina scrambled off the bed and ran to the door but he tackled her to the floor. He tore her panties off with one powerful tug. She tried to crawl away from him but he landed on her again with such force that it took her breath away. Before she could catch her breath, Dominic positioned Krystina on her parted knees, exposing her most intimate parts to his gaze.

He smacked her pussy, catching her by surprise. She whimpered as a jolt of pure bliss raced through her. This wasn't the way things were supposed to be but when he smacked her pussy again she screamed, but this time from pleasure. He pummeled her neither region until she could barely hold herself up.

"You're mine. And don't you forget it!"

She lowered her head, feeling weak because once again she submitted to him. Krystina couldn't move as she heard the sound of him unbuckling his belt. She couldn't move when he grabbed a handful of her hair and shoved his cock deep inside of her wet channel.

"Mine," he growled each time he slammed into her. Even when she reached a mind-blowing orgasm, he continued to plow into her like a man possessed. Krystina collapsed unable to hold herself up. But instead of stopping, he rolled her onto her back and thrust into her. Wrapping his hands around her throat he squeezed, making eye contact as he literally stole her breath away.

"You don't run things, Krystina. I do." He pulled out of her then and then spilled his seed on her body.

When he finally released her, she rolled away from him. For as long as she had known him, Krystina vowed that she would never let him see her cry, but this was one time she couldn't keep her promise because he had finally broken her. Tears ran unheeded down her cheeks and she didn't bother to wipe them away as she curled up into a ball.

He placed his hand on her shoulder. "Krystina..."

She flinched away from him. "Just leave me."

"Look, I—"

"Leave me alone!"

"I went too far."

"You always go too far, so why bring it up now. I can't be around you right now."

"I'm sorry."

The only thing his poor excuse for an apology did was anger her. It gave her the strength to stand up and smack him across the face. "Fuck, your sorry." She turned away from him to grab her robe that hung on the back of the bedroom door.

As she angrily covered herself, she glared at him uncaring that there was now a huge handprint on his face. She hadn't hit anyone since she was a kid when she felt as if she were fighting for her very humanity. "Were you sorry when you were accusing me of putting out for Tyler, and accusing me of flirting with a potential business partner when all I was doing was being friendly and business like? You've gone out of your way to embarrass and humiliate me and to turn my own body against me. But I don't blame you, I place the fault totally at my feet for letting you do it to me. You see, the reason why I left three years ago, wasn't because you kissed me and I didn't like it. I ran away because I liked it too much. I already knew that you would one day reject me just like I've been rejected most of my life. I'm used to it. I was rejected by my father." She broke off on a sob.

"Krystina—"

"No, I'm going to have my say." She paused long enough to compose herself enough to get the words out that needed to be said. "Most people think I have no idea who my father is, but I did. He was some business man my mother was using for money. The problem with that was, he was already married with children. I found out about him when I was younger. My mother showed me his picture. I found his phone number in my mother's things so I called him. We had a long talk about my life and he seemed genuinely interested in it at first. But at the end of the conversation, he told me to never contact him again. And then, there was my mother. She rejected me over and over again, choosing drugs over her own daughter. You have no idea what it's like to have someone come in and out of your life, making promises about doing better and then being disappointed by them time and time again. The last time I saw my mother alive, was on my ninth birthday. My grandmother had given me a fresh twenty dollar bill as a gift. That's a lot of money for a kid who didn't have much. I valued it mainly because I knew my grandmother busted her ass cleaning houses to take care of me and that was a very generous gift from her. My mother disappeared that night, with my twenty dollars."

Fresh tears slid down her face. "I didn't have a lot of friends growing up because I was constantly teased about my drug addict mother, I faced rejection from my peers. Then that storm hit and I was so scared that I was going to die, and part of me kind of wanted to. I was a child and I felt like there was nothing for me. All I had was my grandmother. And then, we got a fresh start. Uncle Charles took us in and I had hope for the first time in a long while. But then, the second you laid eyes on me, I was rejected by you. So, of course, I was angry and fought a lot. I was tired of the world beating on me so I decided to fight back. And despite it all, if you would have shown me the least bit of decency, I would have been your biggest fan. But now, I can't stand the sight of you. Obviously, I won't be going back to the job. This is my official resignation. And before you mention my contract, I dare you to sue me over it. You can show Uncle Charles that picture you have of me. I don't care anymore. If he thinks less of me because of it, then so be it. I've been rejected enough in my life to expect it now. I've gotten past it before and I will again."

With a sigh, she stood up and headed to her bathroom. Krystina glanced over her shoulder to see Dominic standing motionless with all color drained from his face. "I'm going to take a shower now. But when I come back out, I want you gone."

Once she was in the shower, she scrubbed herself trying to rid herself of his scent. Krystina washed her skin until it felt raw. She let the spray of the hot water cascade over her head, allowing it to mingle with her tears. She stayed inside the stall until her skin started to prune.

Finally, when she returned to her room, Dominic was gone but it didn't matter. She couldn't stay here another minute. Quickly she got dressed and gathered her suitcase. Krystina haphazardly threw clothes and the necessary toiletries into it. She then packed up her camera equipment.

Thankfully when she went walked out the house with luggage in hand, Dominic and Uncle Charles weren't around. She took one of the cars in the garage. She made a mental note to have it returned later.

She drove aimlessly in the night, not sure where she'd end up. But, it was as if subconsciously she knew where she was heading all along when she pulled up into a fancy condominium complex. Dragging her belongings with her, she reached door number 18 and rang the doorbell. After several minutes she thought she'd made a wasted trip. "Shit." She muttered under her breath.

Krystina was about to turn around when the door opened and a sleepy-eyed Tyler stood there. "Krystina? What are you doing here?"

"I need a temporary place to stay. Can I stay with you for a few days?"

He crinkled his forehead with obvious confusion but he opened the door wide enough to let her through. "Uh, sure. Come on in."

Chapter Nineteen

"Dominic, I think we did some really great work today. I'm very proud of the progress you've made." Dr. Harlem smiled at him as they concluded the session.

"Thank you," he nodded his head solemnly.

"And just remember, the healing process takes time and it works differently for everyone. Some people are able to move on in a matter of weeks, while others take months. And then, there are some who take years."

"Yeah, like me," he said with a self-deprecating snort.

"Don't beat yourself up about it," she said. "To be perfectly honest there are people who are never able to move and I'm very proud of you for coming back after all this time. I feared when you stopped your visits all those years ago, I would never see you again."

"I thought I was fine, but not after what I did. I can't believe that I..."

"Sometimes in the face of the type of trauma you experienced, people misplace blame instead of where it actually belongs. It was no one's fault except the perpetrator of that horrible crime."

"I know but I felt like it was a betrayal to my mother's memory to..." he broke off unable to say it out loud."

"I understand." Dr. Harlem gave him a sympathetic smile. "And we'll talk some more about that in our next session. Make sure you stop by the front desk to make that appointment. Hopefully, I'll see you next week at the same time."

"Well, actually I'm going away on business next week and then I'm taking some vacation time. But I promise I'll be back."

"I'm glad to hear that you'll be taking some time off. A rested mind is a healthy one."

"Thank you, Dr. Harlem." He stood up and left the room. Before he left the office, he stopped to make an appointment with the office manager for when he returned.

It had been four months since Dominic started seeing the psychologist again. He'd stopped seeing her after he turned 18 because legally his grandfather could no longer make him go and with college, he didn't feel like he could fit therapy sessions in his schedule with all that he had going. Besides, Dominic thought he was just fine. He no longer had the nightmares and he was learning to properly grieve for his mother and the twins.

But then when Miss Willie Mae and Krystina had shown up, he'd been triggered all over again. There were times when he knew he was being unfair to Krystina but he couldn't help himself. It didn't help matters that he'd fallen victim to his family's curse where the Jackson women were concerned. He'd fought against it with every fiber of his being. He hadn't wanted to hurt Krystina as much as he did, but in the end, not only did he break her, he broke himself.

Dominic could barely look at himself in the mirror. He wasn't the only one who seemed to be a having a hard time dealing with him driving Krystina away. When his grandfather had learned that she had left in the middle of the night without a single word of where she was going, he'd stopped speaking to Dominic. It was only recently that the old man was just starting to come around. Even Poppy and Felix, who he could count on for support, were cool toward him. Poppy would shake her head and Felix didn't call him anymore to tell him how his life was going. When Dominic saw his brother, Felix was cordial but there was a wall between them and Dominic had no one to blame but himself.

When he pulled up in the mansion's garage, he was surprised to see both siblings' vehicles parked inside. Neither of them had been home together for a weekend in ages, not since Krystina had left.

With a heavy sigh, he went inside the house, preparing himself for a long night. Sure enough, his grandfather, Poppy, and Felix were in the family room going over brochures. "Am I allowed to ask what everyone is gathered in here for?" He walked into the room hands in pocket.

Poppy rolled her eyes, while Felix kept his gaze firmly planted on the papers in his hands. His grandfather pursed his lips and gave Dominic a narrow-eyed stare before speaking. "The kids and I are planning a vacation. After their finals this week, they have some time off before their summer internships begin."

"Oh? Where were you thinking of going?"

Poppy raised her head with a smirk tilting her lips. "Spain."

"I see." He knew exactly why they were going there and it was their prerogative. "I have business there next week. Maybe it would be better if you three flew with me and I'll have the pilot take you to whichever part you'd like to go to."

"Oh, we'll make do, Dominic. We don't want to inconvenience you. Heaven forbid if that happens," his grandfather replied gruffly.

It was time to end this madness with his family.

"Look, I know the three of you are mad at me and I can't apologize enough, so whatever it is that you want me to do to make things right, I'll do. Just don't be mad at me anymore. I need you guys and I'm sorry I don't tell you enough, but I love each of you. I was a huge asshole and because of that, Krystina suffered for it and as an indirect result, you all did as well."

The room fell silent and no one spoke for several agonizing moments. Dominic wasn't used to apologizing and he wondered if he'd have his apology thrown back in his face. It was no more than he deserved but he had to try. Part of the healing process, according to Dr. Harlem was to make amends to the people he'd hurt.

Felix exhaled deeply as he stood up. "Dom, we're not the ones you should be apologizing to. Sure you were a dick, but we'll get over it. Like you said, we're family and we'll always be here for you. But, Krystina is also family and it's time you accept that."

"I do. I just...you and Poppy remembered what happened but you two were so young at the time and you two had no choice but to stick with the therapy, unlike myself who was too stubborn to continue with it. That isn't an excuse, I'm just letting you know I know why I screwed up and need to fix this. I've been going back to therapy these past few months."

His grandfather straightened up in his seat. "Oh? You never mentioned that."

Dominic smiled without humor. "Well, we all haven't exactly been on speaking terms but I've been going twice a week. I take off early from work on those days and I feel like I'm finally ready to see her."

"Well, it's about damn time," Felix finally spoke up. "Maybe now, you'll finally have the balls to admit your feelings for her."

"You sound as if you know how I feel," Dominic challenged.

Poppy waved her hand dismissively. "Oh, please. We all know you're in love with her. You're the big dumb-dumb who's been in denial all this time. Sure you might have dated several bimbos over the years but none of them ever lasted because deep down you knew Krystina was the one you really wanted."

Even though his siblings were only 19 and 20, at times, they displayed a wisdom beyond their years.

"Felix, Poppy, would you mind excusing yourselves for a minute?" I'd like to speak with Dominic in private."

Felix nodded. "Sure, Grandfather."

Poppy hopped up. "No problem. Don't be too hard on him. I think he's actually sorry."

When his siblings walked past him, they both patted his shoulder in reassuring gestures. It was their way of saying all was forgiven. At least, there was that. He wasn't sure what his grandfather had to say. The expression on the old man's face remained dour.

"Have a seat son." He patted the empty space on the couch that Poppy had vacated.

Dominic sat next to his grandfather. "Thank you."

The old man lifted a bushy gray brow. "For what?"

"For talking to me again."

Charles patted him on the knee. "Dominic, it's not that I wasn't talking to you. The thing is, I wasn't exactly sure what to say to you. You seemed to have had your mind made up about how you wanted to carry on as far as the situation with Krystina went. After I warned you that night about the harm you could be doing and you continued on your path of destruction, there wasn't really much for me to say anymore. You'd made your choice and you had to deal with it. Part of the reason I avoided speaking to you, was because I was feeling a little guilty about the way things had turned out myself."

"How so?"

"Well, like I said in our prior conversation, I never stepped in when I saw how you were toward Krystina but I saw that you were hurting. I figured it would be okay because you weren't around that often when you were in school. And then when I agreed to send Krystina to boarding school, I thought the distance would take care of things. I should have insisted that you continue therapy or, at the very least, forced you to see that you were holding her responsible for something she had no control over. She couldn't help who her mother was. But, I get it. She looks exactly like Candice. And Candice looks liked her mother when she was younger. When I see Krystina, sometimes it's like looking into my past."

"Is that why you wanted to keep her around?"

"Partly. I felt responsible for her mainly because I wanted to make up for what happened to her mother and grandmother. Krystina was my second chance. And even though she was a duty to me in the beginning, I have come to love her very much. She is like my own grandchild and sometimes I wonder, what if?"

Dominic didn't want to judge his grandfather, but he still remembered his grandmother who had been one of the sweetest women he'd met. She'd died from an aggressive form of ovarian cancer when Dominic was nine. Though it was over twenty years ago, he still remembered her sweet smile. It was hard to reconcile that his grandfather had been in love with anyone else. "Did Grandmother know about Miss Willie Mae?"

He sighed. "She did, but you have to understand things were different back then. Don't get me wrong, I loved Millicent to distraction, but Willie always held a special place in my heart. I'm not going to bore you with the long details, but Willie Mae was the daughter of one of the maids in my father's house. He was just starting to get the resort up and running. He wasn't home often and my mother left the raising of me to the help. Me and Willie Mae became friends in a time when that kind of thing was frowned upon. As we grew older, I fell in love with her but we both knew that nothing could ever come of it. If I were a stronger man, I would have fought for us but the thought of being cut off and struggling on my own with a wife, who it was illegal to marry in many states wasn't a prospect I thought I could handle. And, she understood that as well. It was she who insisted that we remain friends."

"Eventually, I went off to college and met your grandmother. She was one of the kindest spirits I knew. I fell for her and eventually made her my wife. Not too long into the marriage, Millicent was pregnant with your father. That's when Willie Mae showed up in my life again, seeking out my help. She'd taken up with some soldier who claimed he would marry her when he came back from his overseas tour during the war. Apparently, when she wrote him to tell him she was pregnant, he sent her a 'Dear Jane' letter. I'm sure you can imagine what it was like for single mothers back in the day. Being the kind-hearted woman she was, Millicent insisted that we take her in. After all, she was very visibly pregnant at the time."

"With Candice?" Dom asked.

Grandfather nodded. "Yes. Willie Mae worked as our main housekeeper and she and Millicent were even friendly, but I always suspected Millicent knew about us although she never said anything. But I was always faithful to your grandmother, except…that one time. You remember that, don't you?"

Dominic nodded. "Yeah, I was over here for a visit when I walked into the kitchen. You and Miss Willie Mae were kissing and from the looks of it, things would have gone further if I hadn't interrupted."

"I know. And I regret you finding out about us that way. I didn't want you to see that. Not that I'm excusing myself, but that was the day I found out your grandmother's cancer diagnosis. I was shattered and so was Willie Mae. Millicent was so brave about it and she was acting like it didn't really matter. She wouldn't allow me to be sad around her. So, I went to Willie Mae to commiserate. I was crying in her arms and then, one thing led to another and you walked in on us. After that was when Willie Mae decided it was time to leave. She had some land in Mississippi left to her by an uncle she didn't know. She thought she could make a go of things down there. Besides, she was worried about Candice and believed a change of scenery would be best for her. I only invited her back into my home when I found out what happened to her and Krystina. With Millicent gone, I thought maybe I'd get a second chance with her. I wanted to wait until she was settled in before I made my move. But then, she died. I'd lost the two loves of my life."

"All this time, I thought that you two had been carrying on an affair behind Grandmother's back. I found it sickening that she'd smile in Grandmother's face while being with you. I resented her a little."

"It's understandable. But like I told you a long time ago, the Holden men's Achilles heel is a Jackson woman. I know you hated Candice but she wasn't really the villain in this story. Your mother wasn't as innocent as you seem to think she was."

Dominic's first instinct was to lose his temper but after months of therapy, he knew that keeping an open mind about things would serve him far better than blowing his top. "I don't understand how my mom was the bad guy. You know what happened to her. She loved my father."

"Of course, she did. I don't dispute that. But, what Susan loved, even more, was the idea of your father. Johnathan was after all the only heir of a very successful empire. Your mother, as sweet as she was, was the type of woman who needed to be taken care of and pampered. I'm not saying that made her bad, but it made her ambitious in the things she wanted. I always kind of thought that Jonathan and Candice would end up together, but then he chose your mother. When I met her, I understood why. Jonathan confessed to me shortly before his death that he'd only married Susan because she told him she was pregnant."

"With me, I assume?"

"No. There was no baby. They eloped because he wanted to do the right thing for his unborn child. But when he discovered that there was no child, it was too late because they'd already married. I do, honestly, believe your father tried to make it work. Then he got tired of trying and he was going to leave her. But, that's when he found out Susan was pregnant for real."

"I believe Jonathan choosing Susan was one of the things that sent Candice spiraling into a bunch of bad stuff. Sometimes, not everything is as it seems, Dominic. I should have told you all this a long time ago, but I didn't want to tarnish your mother's memory. She wasn't a bad person, no one in this story really is, except the bastard who killed her. I'm just sorry that you had to carry all this pain around with you."

Dominic didn't know what to say. Everything he believed to be the truth was a lie. He wanted to be angry, but he couldn't fault his grandfather for keeping it from him. He understood the old man's reasons. And ultimately, it didn't change how he'd treated Krystina. That was all on him. "Just when I didn't think I could feel like a bigger piece of crap, I learn this."

His grandfather patted him on the arm in reassurance. "Don't beat yourself up over this. I believe that you'll fix this."

"But what if she doesn't forgive me?"

"I can't promise that she will. But she's like her grandmother, she has a loving heart. Be prepared for some opposition. She might not be willing to listen right away, but be patient with her. And then there's...." he flushed as he broke off.

"What? Why do I feel like there's something you're not telling me?"

"Well, I didn't want to mention this before, but, I think she might be seeing someone over there. I don't think it's serious or I think she might have said so. Dominic, if you want to win her over. You're going to have a fight on your hands but I think you can do it. I'm pulling for you."

Dominic's heart dropped. Just when he was coming to terms with his true feelings for her, he realized it might be too late. Even if it was, it wouldn't stop him from trying to win her heart because Krystina Jackson was worth fighting for.

Chapter Twenty

The warm Mediterranean sun beat down on her skin. It felt delicious lounging outside on a yacht with a mojito at her side. The lull and scent of the sea had her drifting off to sleep most of the day, but now she was fully alert. Anyone should be happy in these circumstances but something just felt off.

"Will you tell me why such a beautiful woman is wearing such a ferocious frown? Are you not enjoying it out here today?" Tomas asked from beside her. He took her hand in his and brought it to his lips.

She smiled at his concern. He really was a sweetheart and she liked him a lot. Any woman would be lucky to have a man like him. He was probably one of the best-looking men she'd ever seen with his olive complexion, dark bedroom eyes that could seduce a nun, and strong jawline with manicured stubble. Tomas's killer smile alone was probably the very reason why so many women in his company threw themselves at him. And, he'd chosen her. Krystina was flattered by his attention but she couldn't seem to let things go further than some intimate caresses and deep kisses. And through all this Tomas remained a perfect gentleman, not pushing past a point she didn't want to go. She wondered not for the time if she should continue dating him when he obviously felt more for her than she did for him.

This was the second time she had the opportunity to have a healthy relationship with a decent guy who actually seemed to value her as a person, first Tyler and now, Tomas. And it was all because of her masochistic feelings for Dominic. She immediately pushed the thoughts of him from her mind. She refused to let him ruin her day. This was supposed to be a fun day no laptops, cell phones and no talking business.

Krystina turned to smile at the handsome Spaniard. "I didn't realize I was frowning. I guess I was deep in thought."

"If you don't mind me asking, what were you thinking about?"

"I...I'd rather not talk about it if you don't mind."

"Of course. Shall we go in? My chef has prepared a meal for us and I noticed you didn't eat much for breakfast."

Now that she thought about it, she actually could go for something to eat. "Sure. I'm ready." She allowed him to help her off the lounger. He towered over her. Tomas was even taller than Dominic's six feet plus frame. She felt like a dwarf standing next to him.

Tomas led her inside to the dining area and she was surprised with a surplus of seafood dishes such as oysters on a half shell, cracked crab, shrimp and that was only a small portion of what was on the table. She licked her lips in anticipation when she noticed a bowl of ceviche. "Oh my God. How is all this for two people?"

He waved his hand seeming unbothered. "Whatever we don't finish, the crew will have. Have a seat, my dear."

A steward appeared next to the table and proceeded to fill their plates with whatever they requested. When they were alone again, Krystina dug in. "This food is amazing. You went all out today, Tomas."

He gave a small smile before consuming his own meal.

Again the feeling of something being off struck her. She should have been happy. It had been four months since she'd left the US to work in Spain. After she left the mansion, she'd gone to Tyler's apartment. Being the sweetheart he was, Tyler said that she could stay as long as she wanted.

She'd stayed in bed for a solid 24 hours without even turning over. At one point, Tyler had come to check on her to make sure she was still alive. She'd cried on his shoulder and spilled her heart out to him wishing that he was the man she loved instead of Dominic who didn't deserve her love. Tyler had been compassionate and understanding but he'd always been firm, telling her that she would eventually have to get her shit together and face the world again because it would continue to go on without her.

Krystina had taken those words to heart. Knowing that she could never go back to the mansion, she formulated a plan to support herself. She'd managed to build a nice savings for herself having lived rent free for the time she lived at the mansion and worked at Holden's. She figured it shouldn't be hard to find a job with her skills. In the meantime, she could help Tyler pay the bills and rent to ease the burden of her stay. As she was rummaging through her things, she found Tomas's business card. It was like the heavens had given her a sign. She called him and though his assistant had answered for him, she'd assured, Krystina that Tomas would return her call when he was able.

She had been surprised when he'd called her back the very next day and was eager for her to come on board to work as one of his tourism liaisons. He'd assured her he'd be able to pull some strings to get her work visa in order by the end of the week. And, he'd been good on his word.

Krystina found herself on a plane as soon as she got word. She'd only called Uncle Charles, Poppy, and Felix to let them know that she was okay and what her plans were but other than that, she couldn't bear to see any of them in person. She was scared that they'd convince her to stay and she couldn't do it. Not when she'd be in such close proximity to Dominic.

Her job with the Sandoval involved a little marketing and dealing with groups from all over the world who wanted to use their services. She even had her own assistant. The best part about it, travel was involved. What she didn't count on was catching Tomas's eye. When he'd asked her out she'd politely declined, but he'd persisted until finally, she agreed to have dinner with him one night. On their first date, they'd eaten dinner at an authentic Moroccan restaurant. Afterward, they'd gone dancing which was followed by a long walk on the beach.

From that point on, they'd fallen into a dating pattern where he'd take her out when she wasn't swamped with work. Tomas would take her to fancy engagements where she rubbed elbows with the elite. Anyone would have said that she was living a dream come true. But like now, she was simply going through the motions. She wasn't sure what to call what she and Tomas had. Krystina enjoyed his company and always had a good time when they were together but she didn't know if she'd ever see him as more than a friend she occasionally made out with.

Krystina was halfway done with the food on her plate before she realized that Tomas was unusually silent. Since she'd known him, he was always quite loquacious telling her about his many adventures. "Now, it's my turn to ask. Is everything okay?"

Again, he gave her a faint smile. "This isn't going to work is it?"

"Excuse me? What are you talking about?"

"You and I? This thing we have, it's not going to progress beyond what it is."

Unable to meet his gaze, she looked down at her food. "I'm sorry."

"*Cara*, look at me."

She raised her head tears stinging the backs of her eyes. "I'm sorry."

"Why are you crying?"

"Because you've been so nice to me and I wish I could return your feelings for me. It's just..."

"I understand. Your heart belongs to another. I should have left well enough alone but you're far too lovely a temptation to resist." He gave her a sad smile. "What can I say? I like a challenge but despite my reputation with the ladies, I am a man of honor. I gave this my best shot but I knew I was defeated about ten minutes ago."

"What do you mean?"

"I've wined and dined you and have taken you to the best restaurants. We've gone places where most people won't see in a lifetime. We're out in the middle of the sea on my yacht but the most excitement you've shown so far today was for the food."

"Tomas, I'm having a good time. Really, I am." She sighed. "I like spending time with you."

"But not in a romantic way."

"I'm sorry. I wish..."

"Don't apologize. The heart wants what the heart wants. No matter what happens, I'm glad that we can at least walk away from this with a beautiful friendship."

"I wish things could have been different."

"As do I. So, I'm to assume things didn't work out with you and Mr. Holden?"

She sighed. There was really no point in denying it. "There really wasn't anything to work out. We weren't really a thing."

"Oh? So I imagined you coming back downstairs to join us that day with disheveled clothes? Don't look so surprised, *cara*. I've been with many women in my lifetime and I know when one has been freshly fucked."

Krystina couldn't remember the last time she felt this embarrassed. She smacked her forehead with her palm. "Oh, God. I can't believe you noticed that."

He grinned broadly. "You cleaned yourself up pretty good for the most part. If I wasn't so well versed in the ways of love, I might not have noticed. Sometimes when passion takes over, it doesn't matter where you are when it happens. So that brings me back to my original question, what happened between you and Holden? Is he the reason you decided to work for me? Was it to spite him?"

"Actually no. I mean I wanted to work over here because I needed to get away from him. A person can only take so much before they've had enough. I've been putting up with Dominic's brand of disdain for years. Shortly before our trip to Ibiza, things changed. He'd do things to me that...well, I won't go into detail, but I liked it. Maybe that's why I fooled myself into believing that it was something more. I feel like such an idiot."

Tomas reached across the table and took her hand in his. "You're not an idiot. We've all played the fool for love. But may I share some of my observations?"

She shrugged. "Can I stop you?"

Tomas grinned. "No. But anyway, whenever I observed the two of you when neither of you realized I was watching, I noticed the longing looks you'd give him. And when I observed Holden, I saw the lust in his eyes, but it wasn't just pure desire. There was something more there. There was also conflict. I could see that he didn't want to feel it but he was in love with you."

"You could tell all that just by observing us?"

"Absolutely. Why else do you think he got so jealous whenever the two of us talked? I noticed that, too. Look, Krystina, I know this isn't my business but I hate seeing you so sad. You've been in a lot of pain these past months you've worked at Sandoval group and I was hoping to put that light back into your eyes, but I've failed. Regardless of what happens between you and Holden, you're never going to truly be able to move on until you face him again."

Even though she wanted to deny it, she recognized the wisdom in his words. "The only way that's going to happen is if I got back to the states. I don't think I'm ready to go back yet."

"You won't have to."

"What do you mean?"

"I didn't tell you about it at first because I wanted to see if I had a genuine chance with you."

She pulled her hand away from his. "You're hedging. Spit it out."

"I'll be heading back to Ibiza for another meeting with Holden and his group. He's coming next week and because of your knowledge of Holden's inner workings, I was going to ask you to come with me. It's not essential. You only have to come if you want to. If you don't, you can teleconference into the meetings. So, Krystina…will you come?"

Chapter Twenty-One

"Krystina!"

She turned when she heard her name yelled in the lobby of Holden's resort in Ibiza. Krystina braced herself when Poppy launched herself into her arms. "Whoa," she laughed. "You almost knocked me down. Maybe you should consider becoming a professional football player." Krystina hugged the younger girl with enthusiasm.

"Hey, Krystina." Felix gave her a more relaxed hug once his sister let go. "How's it going?"

"Pretty good. I'm so glad to see the two of you."

"And where's my hug?" Uncle Charles said from the rear as he approached her.

Tears sprang to her eyes as she saw the man who'd been like a father to her. She went into his embrace and wept with joy. "I missed you so much."

"If I would have known I'd get this kind of reception, I would have come sooner." He pulled away and gently wiped her tears away.

"I'm sorry for leaving the way I did, but I had to do it."

"Shh, no need to apologize. I understand. Shall we go to our suite?"

Krystina nodded as she followed her family to their accommodations.

After a lot of soul-searching, she decided to take the trip from Madrid to Ibiza with Tomas, if for nothing else to get closure with Dominic. To her surprise, however, shortly after agreeing to take the journey, she received a call from Uncle Charles informing her that he, Poppy and Felix would be flying in with Dominic and they wanted to meet up before she was stuck in business meetings.

Tomas suggested she spend the day with her family before seeing Dominic so he gave her the day off while Dominic met with the Sandoval group on Tomas' estate. She appreciated the chance to spend some time with Uncle Charles, Felix, and Poppy.

Once they were in their suite, all three Holdens bombarded Krystina with questions about the last four months of her life. She laughed. "Okay, one at a time. Yes, I'm really enjoying my job. I've met a lot of interesting people and I feel like my language skills have improved tremendously. I've been working on my Portuguese since the Sandoval Group has an office there as well."

"And what about you and Tomas Sandoval? I saw you on a gossip blog together. You looked great. Is he as hot in person as he is in pictures?" Poppy asked.

"Tomas and I are just friends. We did date for a little while, but it didn't work out."

"So does that mean he's single?" Poppy followed up.

"I think you need a dip in the pool to cool off, Pop," Felix teased his sister.

"I was just asking. A girl can try."

"What happened to that guy you were dating, Poppy?" Krystina wondered.

"Oh, we're done. He was way too clingy. He was talking about marriage and we haven't even dated for a year. Besides, I want to finish school before I settle down."

"That's a wise decision," Uncle Charles added to the conversation.

The conversation veered toward what Krystina had been up to these past months whenever she wasn't working. She told them about the book of photos she was working on in her spare time. Krystina asked Felix and Poppy about their upcoming summer internships. They then discussed Uncle Charles' charity work. To give himself something to do the old man had started working with a nonprofit that helped families in need. The four of them talked about anything and everything without addressing the elephant in the room. Dominic. It felt good seeing them again. Their visit was just what she needed to lift her spirits. This was her family. For so long, she didn't feel like she belonged because she was made to feel unworthy, but she realized she loved these people with all her heart. It didn't matter that they were from different backgrounds. They loved each other and that was all that mattered.

They had a meal prepared for them by the concierge and by the time Krystina was ready to go back to house Tomas's rental property, it was late. Time had really flown. They'd made plans to get together again before they left the island.

As she headed toward the lobby, Krystina called the car service to come pick her up. She didn't mind waiting outside for it because the weather was nice and she liked to people watch. As she sat by the valet stand, one of the resort's official vehicles pulled up a few feet away from her. The chauffeur got out of the car first and went to open the door for the passenger in the back. The windows were tinted so she couldn't see who was inside.

She started scrolling through emails on her phone and was so focused, she didn't hear anyone approach.

"Krystina?"

She looked up and froze. Standing in front of her was Dominic.

Dominic thought he was imagining things when he spotted Krystina sitting on a bench looking at her phone. Though she was slightly thinner, she was just as beautiful as he remembered. Her hair was around her shoulders in a big puffy afro. Her skin seemed a bit darker, probably from being out in the sun, but it suited her. The colorful sundress she wore made she skin glow like the goddess she was.

As he moved closer, he realized it was her. His heart began to beat fast. He didn't think he'd see her today. It took everything within him to not race over to her and throw himself at her feet. Dominic had learned Krystina was working for Sandoval from his grandfather and he'd half expected her to be at the meeting today. He'd even swallowed his pride and asked Sandoval in private if she'd be joining them anytime that week and had been informed that she would but today she was taking a private day.

The news had filled him with joy and fear. He would get to see Krystina sooner than he anticipated. Dominic was nervous, but now she was here and he wasn't going to lose this opportunity. Taking a deep breath, he approached her. "Krystina."

She looked up and her eyes widened in surprised. "Dominic!" Slowly she stood. "Uh, I didn't think we'd run into each other today."

"Neither did I, but things went so smoothly today we were able to wrap up ahead schedule. So, I take it you were here to see Grandfather, Poppy, and Felix."

"Yes, I was very happy to see them."

"Why are you sitting out here?"

"Just waiting for the car to come pick me up."

Dominic opened his mouth to speak but the words wouldn't come. As the awkward silence stretched between them, he cursed internally. Why was it so hard for him to get the words out? He wanted to tell her how he felt but realized that would be going way too fast. Not wanting to miss this opportunity, he blurted out. "Have dinner with me."

She stared at him blankly for several seconds before answering. "I already ate."

"Then, have a drink with me or whatever. I think it's time we had a talk. We don't have to go to my suite. We can go to one of the private lounges and just talk. I promise. I feel that there's so much I need to tell you, and so much that you deserve to know."

Again, she took a long pause before answering. Over these last four months, Krystina must have mastered how to mask her feelings because he couldn't tell what she was thinking. She released a deep breath. "Okay. Let me cancel the car service."

He was actually surprised that she agreed. Dominic had half expected her to spit in his face. It wouldn't have been more than he deserved.

Once she'd sorted her transportation issue out, he led her to his private lounge. "Would you like me to order you a drink?"

She shook her head. "No, thank you. I'd rather just get this conversation over with. You know, I'm actually glad we could meet up."

Dominic raised a brow in shock. "Really? I thought you would never talk to me again."

"The thought did cross my mind, but I wouldn't have been able to move on with my life and not think about the what ifs. This way, I can get the closure I need."

At the mention of the word closure his heart tightened. It sounded so final. Maybe she thought it was over, but he didn't intend to back down without a fight because she was worth fighting for. He only wished that he'd realized this before he'd run her off.

"Before you say anything else Krystina, I want you to know that what I did to you was inexcusable. I allowed my past and my jealousy to rule my head. I refused to acknowledge my true feeling for you until it was too late."

Krystina maintained a poker face. "And how do you feel about me?"

"I'm in love with you. I think I loved you for a long time but I was too stubborn to admit it. I was too busy trying not to repeat the mistakes I thought my grandfather and father had made."

She let out a humorless laugh. "You have a funny way of showing it, Dominic. I'm not exactly sure what your father and Uncle Charles have to do with anything. You were the one who made my life a living hell, not them."

"I'd gladly walk through the pits of hell to right the wrongs that I've done."

"I just want to know why? What is this past you keep bringing up and why was I the one who had to pay the price?"

"If you'll bear with me, I'll tell you everything. It's a pretty long and complicated story, some of which I've only learned recently."

She shrugged. "I'm in no rush to get back to my place. Tell me."

He raked his hands through his hair and exhaled heavily. "Do you remember when I was telling you that I hated taking pictures because they lie?"

"Yes."

"Well, as I said before, I thought I had one happy family. It was me, my father and mother. I was just a kid and I didn't know things weren't what they appeared to be. I was oblivious to the tension between my parents. And then, the arguments started. They fought all the time. And the common theme seemed to be Candice. I heard that name often when my parents would argue. It was Miss Willie Mae's daughter, your mother. I remember seeing her around at my grandfather's when I was younger, but then she and Miss Willie Mae left. I didn't see them again until Candice would randomly pop up. It's my understanding that Miss Willie Mae and Candice had moved to Mississippi but Candice must have come back to renew a relationship with my father."

"While he was still married to your mother?"

"Yes."

"You said renew. Are you saying that they had something together before he and your mother were married?"

"Apparently. But like I said before, some of this story I've only learned recently myself from my grandfather. In my mind, your mother was someone who was tearing my family apart. She was the woman who made my mother cry every night. When I said she started popping up, I remember this one time when my mother went out of town for one of her sorority get-togethers and it just me and my father. On the second night, my mother was gone, I saw her. I woke up to the sound of voices. I went downstairs and I saw my father and Candice, making love on the couch. I was so young I didn't fully understand what they were doing, but I knew it was wrong. I didn't know what to do, so I ran back up to my room without neither of them noticing that I'd seen them."

"Oh my God," Krystina whispered. "I had no idea."

"You couldn't have and I shouldn't have held you responsible for it, but let me get this all off my chest."

"Okay."

"It happened again. When my mother wasn't around and he thought I was sleeping he would bring Candice into our home. I was too scared to mention what I'd seen to my mother and I didn't know why at the time."

"On some psychological level, you were probably trying to protect her. Kids tend to show loyalty to their parents in that way."

"That's what my therapist said. That's very observant of you."

"I took a few psychology courses in college. That's pretty amateur stuff."

"I guess." Dominic sighed before continuing. "The last time I remember seeing Candice was when I was about seven, nearly eight. I remember it just like yesterday. We were having dinner and the doorbell rang. My Dad went to answer the door. Candice came storming into the house and confronted my mother. She said that she was pregnant and the baby was my father's. She seemed distraught, not like I remembered her. She was rail thin and there were huge dark circles under her eyes. She looked like she'd been sleeping on the street. My father tried to calm her down and told her the baby couldn't be his because he hadn't seen her in months. That semi-confession sent my mother into hysterics. It was a big mess. My mother packed her bags that night and took me with her. We ended up staying with an old boyfriend of hers."

Krystina frowned. "Was my mother actually pregnant or did she just say that to break your parents up?"

"Yes, she was pregnant with you."

"Oh." She scrunched her head in confusion. "Well, obviously, we're not brother and sister. I've talked to my father before."

"No, we're not. Like my father had said, he hadn't seen her in months. By that time, she might have gotten involved with some unsavory people hence her appearance. She probably found herself pregnant and went to the first person she thought she could get money out of."

"But your parents must have reconciled because of Poppy and Felix."

"They never got back together. My mother remarried that old boyfriend of hers. Poppy and Felix are my half-brother and sister."

Krystina gasped. "I...I didn't know. You all look so much alike."

"I have my father's coloring but we all favor my mother. I can only assume my dad didn't take up with Candice again because I never saw her again. But I blamed her for breaking up my family and for everything that happened afterward. My father started drinking heavily and one night he had a little too much and crashed his car into a tree. His airbag didn't deploy and he was killed instantly."

"I'm sorry."

He shrugged. "Honestly, I feel like I'd lost him long before he died. When Candice disappeared I think she took his life essence with her, he wasn't the same man. I was mourning him before he died in that car accident. My father was no saint, but my stepfather was a nightmare. He was abusive and used me and my mother as punching bags. Once, he blacked both of my eyes and cracked a couple of my teeth. My mother was too afraid to take me to the hospital because she thought Gary, my stepfather, would punish us even worse. I missed a month of school. I wasn't even allowed to see Grandfather."

"That's awful. And did he hurt Poppy and Felix?"

"My mother and I tried to protect them the best we could. Gary had a short temper and was violent. Our entire family was held hostage. Shortly, after my mother gave birth to Poppy, she got pregnant again. I think the idea of supporting more kids must have set Gary off because he became more abusive. He was an investment broker but I think he believed his career should have progressed further than it had. He'd take those frustrations out on us. When I got older, I started hitting the gym and taking boxing classes. I was about fifteen when I started fighting back. One day, he just sucker punched me for no reason and I kicked his ass. He never messed with me again, but later that night he took it out on my mother. I never touched him again. I begged my mother to leave him. I told her that my grandfather would take us all in but she made excuses for Gary and told me things would get better. Once Gary knew that I could stand up for myself, he pretty much left me alone. He even backed off mom and the kids when I was around. By that time, Mom had twins. A boy and a girl, Gary Jr. and Andrea. After they were born, I felt it was my duty to protect them somehow. I couldn't let them grow up in the hell that me, Felix and Poppy were in, so I reconnected with my grandfather and I explained to him what was going on. Grandfather filed paperwork to get custody of me. And though he didn't have legal rights to Poppy, Felix and the twins, he filed for guardianship of them as well."

"Dominic," Krystina whispered. "What happened to Gary Jr. and Andrea?"

His chest grew tight as he thought about his baby siblings. They were far too young for what happened to them. "I, um, I was pretty much living with grandfather by that time but one day I just had this premonition of sorts that something wasn't right. It was the night before the preliminary hearing of the custody case. I went to check on my mother and when I got to the door, I heard a gunshot."

"Oh no!"

Dominic paused as he relived that night, trying to hold back the tears he thought he was no longer capable of shedding. "I circled around the house and went to the side entrance and eased my way into the house. I heard screaming from upstairs. I raced into the direction of the voices and I saw Gary standing over the twins' cribs My mother was screaming hysterically. The gun was smoking and it didn't take much for me to put together what had happened."

Krystina's eye widened in horror. "He killed them."

Dominic nodded, not trusting himself to speak

Krystina reached across the table and gripped his hand. "I'm so sorry."

He shook his head. "Don't...don't apologize," he managed to finally get the words out. "Gary was so busy yelling and taunting my mother that he didn't see me. I had to check on Poppy and Felix. I found them in Felix's room. Hiding under their bed. I got them out of the house as quickly as I could. I got them into my car and drove away. As soon as I could, I called the police but by the time they got there, Gary had shot my mother and turned the gun on himself. To this day, I wonder if I could have saved her."

"You can't beat yourself up over that."

"But I can't help but think that if I hadn't at least tried, she'd be alive today."

"There's no telling what the outcome could have been. For all you know, he could have killed you, too. However, one thing you do know for certain is that Poppy and Felix are alive today because of your quick thinking."

He wiped away a tear, embarrassed at his show of emotion. "I blamed your mother for what happened to my family because she was an easy target to focus my hatred on. After my mother died, my grandfather took in Poppy and Felix. He gained full custody of them because my mother's family weren't willing to raise them, but they certainly wanted a hefty payout to stay out of their lives. My grandfather even gave them his last name so they could feel a part of the family. He never treated them any differently than me because that's the kind of man he is. But then you and your grandmother came along, and you looked just like your mother. All those emotions came flowing back. I was an asshole and I'm sorry I treated you the way I did. I was in so much pain that I lashed out at you because it was the easy thing to do."

"I see. There's something else you kind of hinted at in a previous conversation. Was there something between my Uncle Charles and my Grandmother?"

He nodded. "Yes, but that's his story to tell and I'm sure he will one day."

"Okay, "Krystina said quietly as she clenched her hands in her lap and wouldn't look up. "You hurt me really bad, Dominic. Against my better judgment, I fell in love you and not just because of the sex. I saw something in you that was special. I could see it in the way you interacted with Felix, Poppy and Uncle Charles. I saw it at work. On our trip when we talked, I felt a connection. But then you treated me like a possession and it's going to take some time for me to get past that. I do, however, appreciate you sharing everything with me. I forgive you, Dominic, but it'll be hard for me to forget."

"I understand."

She continued to look down at her lap and didn't speak for several minutes. He wasn't sure what she was thinking but the longer the silence stretched, the more nervous he became. Unable to help himself, he had to ask, "Krystina? Do you still love me?"

Chapter Twenty-Two

"Krystina, my dear. So glad you can join me today before we head to the airport." Uncle Charles smiled at her when the concierge led her into the suite. This was the final day of his vacation with Poppy and Felix and he'd invited her over for breakfast. Tomas had generously allowed her the morning off so she could see her family off to the airport.

"Good morning, Uncle Charles." She leaned over and kissed him on the cheek. "Where's Poppy and Felix?"

"They're having breakfast in the restaurant downstairs. I actually wanted to get you alone and have a conversation."

"Sound ominous," she murmured as she took a seat at the dining room table.

"Nothing too heavy. I just wanted to see your face before I left. We haven't had a nice talk for a while."

"Uncle Charles, you know I love you, right?"

"Of course, I do. Why would you ask that?"

"Because, I can usually tell when you have something weighing on your mind. I haven't seen you look like this since you informed me I'd be going to be boarding school."

A pensive look entered his eyes and he released a sigh. "You always were perceptive. Actually, I wanted to ask you how things are going with you and Dominic?"

Krystina wasn't sure how to answer that question because she didn't know the answer herself. After her talk with Dominic, she left him without answering his final question. She had a lot to think through. Working with him this past week had been awkward, but they were cordial toward each other. Every now and then, she'd catch him staring at her with a look of longing that made her heart skip a beat. Part of her wanted to tell him that she still loved him. But the other half warned her to be cautious. She understood that he was getting help for his past issues, but she had her own issues to work out as well.

"I've only seen him in a business setting so things have been fine."

"But what about the talk you had with him a few nights again? Don't look so surprised, he told me about it."

Krystina didn't have any intentions of divulging that conversation to Uncle Charles, but now that he knew there was no point in remaining secretive about it. "He told me about what happened to his mother. That's terrible what happened to her and the twins."

"Yes. Dominic adored his mother. He's always carried this guilt around about not being able to save her. I think because of the history between my son and your mother, he believed that he was betraying Susan's memory by being with you. Anyone with eyes could see that Dominic was smitten with you. But you're the spitting image of your mother so that added to the guilt. I know it sounds crazy but sometimes we hurt the ones we're with so we don't have to deal with the underlying issues and Dominic had plenty of them."

"I feel bad for what my mother did."

"Your mother isn't to blame. My son was right there along with her, but as I was telling Dominic, his mother wasn't the innocent he thought she was. Candice and Henry were an item long before Susan came into the picture. I think Susan was a sweet girl, but she had avarice in her heart and I do believe she set out to have Henry by any means necessary. I think when she was successful at seducing Henry away from Candice, that's when your mother's life took a turn in the wrong direction. And I'm pretty sure that Dominic has already figured out that Susan was seeing his stepfather, Gary, before she and my son separated. I'm not telling you this to paint her as the villain. I'm just trying to demonstrate that life is complicated as are people and a lot of players in the drama were responsible for making this fiasco happen."

"It's so much to wrap my head around."

"Understandable. If I hadn't played a small part, I wouldn't quite get it either. I should have protected you better when you were younger."

"You did a fantastic job, and I didn't expect you to go against your own grandson on my behalf."

"But that's where you're wrong because you're just as much my grandchild as he is. Just as Poppy and Felix might not be my blood, my love for them couldn't be any stronger if they were. I just thought things would eventually get better."

"He was never outright rude around you and honestly looking back, sure he said some things that shouldn't have come out of his mouth, but I think the worst part was when he would shut me out."

"Probably because he didn't want to feel anything for you. In the beginning, it was most likely because he resented you for being your mother's daughter. Keep in mind that he'd only lost his mother a few years prior to you and your grandmother coming to live with us. Then as you grew older and he started developing feelings beyond animosity toward to you, he probably became even more disagreeable."

"I never suspected that was the reason. I just figured he was being his hateful self, but when we talked, it cleared a lot of things up. When I left to go overseas that first time, Dominic showed me that he was interested in me but in a romantic way. So I fled. And when I came back, he was even more aggressive. But every time we were together, I fell for him a little more. Does that make me crazy?"

"No. It makes you human. Maybe us Holden men are just as much of a weakness for the Jackson women as they are to us."

She nodded. "It's quite possible." Krystina paused before broaching what was probably a sensitive top for the old man. "Dominic told me that you and my grandmother…"

Uncle Charles tilted his head heavenward and let out a heavy sigh before turning his steady gaze on Krystina once more. "It's true. I loved your grandmother and if the time had been different, I probably would have married her. But then I met my Millicent and she helped me to move on and have a good life, even though I never quite got over Willie Mae. During the entirety of our marriage I remained faithful to my wife except for one indiscretion with your grandmother, Dominic caught us. I'm not proud of myself but you have the right to know. When Millicent died and a respectable amount of time had passed, I reached out to your grandmother, but she was raising you and having a difficult time with Candice disappearing and reappearing into your lives. She didn't think it was a good idea to come back and stir up past things that were better left alone. Her words, not mine."

"Wow. No wonder Dominic saw the women in my family as some kind of she-devil seductresses."

"I'd like to think fate played a hand in bringing you to us to right two generations of wrongs. Henry and I couldn't get it right with Willie Mae and Candice. And, Dominic has certainly done a fine job of screwing things up, but dare I say that there might be hope? Every time I speak with him, all he can talk about is you. Am I being too intrusive to ask if you return my grandson's feelings?"

Caught off guard by the question, she nearly spit out the coffee she'd been in the process of sipping.

"Are you all right?"

"Yes. I guess I wasn't expecting you to ask me that question."

"I won't lie to you, Krystina. I wouldn't mind you and Dominic making a go of things, but I know that how he treated you might be a little hard for you to get past. You don't have to answer my question, but I just want you to know whatever you decide, I'll support you."

It was good to know she had Uncle Charles in her corner. She didn't know how she would have survived her formative years without him. "Thank you."

He reached across the table and patted her hand. "The pleasure has been all mine. You've become an extraordinary young lady and I'm very proud of you and I know your grandmother would have been, too."

"Uncle Charles?" she began hesitantly.

"I do still love him. But, I'm scared."

"I believe that should conclude our business for now. Our group will be visiting the states for the next meeting." Tomas Sandoval stood up and walked over to Dominic to shake his hands. The rest of the associates followed suit.

When it was Krystina's turn, he held on to her hand a little longer than he should have but he couldn't help it. As soon as their hands touched, he felt a jolt of electricity. The spark was still there. Dominic was almost certain he didn't imagine it and judging from the way she snatched her hand away from his, Krystina had felt it too.

This was the final day of their business week which officially commenced his vacation. He intended to spend it in Spain, close to Krystina. As the rest of the businessmen dispersed, Krystina was at the rear of her group. Dominic caught her by the wrist to halt her progress. She turned to face him with an exasperated sigh.

"What do you want Dominic?"

"I'd like to see you."

"You're seeing me now."

He shook his head. "Not in a business capacity. I want to take you out. I screwed things up with up before but I want to do things right this time around."

She sighed. "Dominic, you're working under the assumption that there's going to be a 'this' time and second, I'm going back to Madrid with my team, later this afternoon. You have to go back home I'm sure."

"Actually, I don't. I'm taking a vacation for the first time in years. I've rented a villa in Madrid where I'll be staying for the next month."

She crinkled her nose. "Why?"

"To be closer to you. When I asked you if you were still in love with me, you didn't say yes. But, you didn't say no either so I'm holding on to that hope that there's something there. Please. I'd like a chance for us to see what could happen when I'm not acting completely insane."

She took a step away from him. "Dominic…I don't know. Look I won't lie, I still have feelings for you. But the way things happened, I'm frightened that you're going to turn on me again. What if you look at me and you can't get past the fact that I look like my mother or if I even look at another guy you won't go completely berserk? I can't live my life in fear."

"You're right, you don't know, but I'd like to show you how things can be between us." He stepped closer. "How they should be." Dominic captured her chin between his thumb and forefinger and dipped his head to lightly brush her lips with his. It took everything within him not to get a proper taste but he needed to take things slow and do things properly.

"Okay," she finally answered. "But just know that things aren't going to be like they were before. They can't be."

"Of course not. If I could take back what I did, would, but I'm going to spend the rest of my life making it up to you."

Krystina gave him the first genuine smile in a long time. "I'm going to hold you to that."

"Why are you so nervous? It's just Dominic. No one special," Poppy rolled her eyes through Krystina's laptop. Krystina video chatted with Poppy and Felix at least once a week. Sometimes, she got to talk to Uncle Charles via webcam but one of his grandkids had to be there to help him set it up. She'd been back in Madrid for two weeks and true to his word, Dominic had appeared on her doorstep the very night she was all settled. He'd taken her to a nightclub with live music. It was too loud to talk, but they didn't need to. Instead, they'd danced, and she found herself enjoying it.

The following night, he'd taken her for a long stroll around town. And again, they didn't do too much talking but Krystina enjoyed their time nonetheless. Each night, he took her somewhere different and she found herself eagerly anticipating when he'd come back. On her day off, they'd had a day trip exploring the city. Krystina had, of course, taken her camera but to her surprise, Dominic had a camera of his own. He'd wanted her to show him how to work the equipment and take a good picture. That was probably her favorite date. She was really starting to relax around him and just enjoy his company for what it was. And on all their outings, he didn't touch her beyond a perfunctory kiss on the cheek when they parted.

Last night, Dominic told her that he wanted to take her somewhere special but wouldn't disclose where.

"I know you don't mean that," Krystina laughed.

"I know but you're running around your room as if you're about to meet the King of Spain. So what's so special about tonight?" Poppy asked.

"I'm not sure. Your brother won't tell me."

Poppy grinned. "Hmm, maybe he's going to ask you to marry him."

"God, I hope not. It's way too soon and things are far too complicated with us right now."

"I thought the two of you were getting along well."

"It's only been a couple weeks. Just because I might have feelings for your brother doesn't mean it's going to erase the past. I'm giving him this chance more for myself than for him. I don't want to spend the rest of my life wondering 'what if'."

"I thought you were giving him a chance because you forgave him."

"I do forgive him but it doesn't mean Dominic doesn't have to put in the work. I get that his past warped how he viewed things, but sometimes sorry doesn't automatically put things back together. It takes time and hard work. I'm glad Dominic is putting the work in and he understands what he has to do."

"But, are you putting in the work?"

Krystina frowned. "What do you mean?"

"If there's any chance of the two of you making a go at a real relationship, you have to do your part as well. Sure, you can let him take you out and romance you. However, if you're just going through the motions just to say you gave it a shot to absolve you from any guilt, then you're not really being genuine."

Krystina opened her mouth to protest but stopped. Was she doing that to Dominic? She was going out with him regularly, but was she really giving him her all?

She looked at her laptop screen to see Poppy giving her a smug look. "Cat got your tongue?"

"Uh, I'm not really sure what to say to that."

"Look, Krystina, I'm not trying to come down on you. Just making an observation. I won't lie and say I'm not rooting for the two of you to work things out because it will make my grandfather happy and Dominic. And, I think it would make you happy, too, if you allow it."

"For a 19-year-old, you're pretty profound."

Poppy grinned. "Hey, I'm an old soul. Okay, hate to cut this conversation short but I have to go. I have a dentist appointment. I hate going but I've grown rather fond of my teeth."

Krystina giggled. "I know the sentiment. Give Uncle Charles a kiss for me and tell Felix to call me. I haven't heard from him in a week."

"Oh, he's wrapped up in a new relationship. No one has heard from him. You know how new love can be. I'm sure you'll hear from him eventually. Okay, I'll catch you later...sis." Poppy winked before ending the connection.

"Bye, Poppy."

It took a few minutes after the conversation was over before the last thing Poppy said sunk in. She seriously doubted Dominic would propose, especially when she wasn't ready to accept. But Poppy's other words were actually worth examining. Krystina really thought she was giving Dominic a fair chance, but there were times when she held back. She didn't laugh as loud as she wanted or when there was something she wanted to tell him, she held back. She thought it was just being cautious but was she really holding back to punish Dominic without even realizing it?

Chapter Twenty-Three

Dominic approached Krystina's apartment. He couldn't remember the last time he'd been this nervous. Since he'd began spending his time with Krystina, he thought he was actually making progress but there were times when she seemed closed off and he wasn't sure what was going on. He feared that it might be because she hadn't truly forgiven him. He understood that it would be a process to win her over, and he'd continue to do whatever it took to make that happen. It was just that he was scared that one day she'd realize she no longer wanted to give him a shot. That thought had weighed heavily on his mind.

His vacation was nearing an end and he hoped after tonight he knew where he stood as far as she was concerned. It was why he had something extra special planned for her. Taking a deep breath, he knocked on her door.

When Krystina answered the door, he froze. Standing in a simple white strapless mini dress that made her dark skin glow, she was absolutely breathtaking. Her hair was piled on top of her head in a big puff and the only jewelry she wore were a pair of pearl drop earrings. She had the type of ethereal beauty that would last well into her twilight years. Dominic had the sudden urge to pull her into her arms and plant kisses along her bare shoulders and collar bone.

"Hi, Dominic. I'll go grab my purse and we can go."

He suddenly remembered the floral arrangement he was holding. "Uh, I brought you these."

She gave him a shy smile. "Thank you. I love them. I didn't realize roses came in lavender. Why don't you come in while I put these in water? How did you choose purple?"

"Because I know that it's your favorite color."

Her eyes widened.

"Don't look so surprised. I pay attention. Anything that relates to you is important to me." She took a step closer, closing the distance between them. Dominic cupped the side of her face and gave her cheek a soft caress.

She backed away abruptly. "I...I uh. Thank you. I'll be right back." Krystina scurried off to the kitchen.

Dominic cursed himself for being too forward. He'd promised himself that he'd let Krystina set the pace but it had been difficult for him to keep his hands to himself. She was just so beautiful. And the scent of her floral-scented perfume was intoxicating.

When she returned with a purse in hand, she smiled. "Let's go."

On their way to their destination, they rode in silence for several minutes just listening to the soft music playing in the background. Krystina was the first to speak. "Dominic, where are you taking me?"

"If I told you, it wouldn't be a surprise."

"The suspense is killing me."

"We'll be there soon enough. Relax and enjoy the ride."

Twenty minutes later, they pulled into the driveway of his villa.

Krystina frown as she looked at her surroundings. "Where are we? This looks like a private residence."

"This is actually where I've been staying these past weeks. I have something special planned."

Krystina seemed a bit apprehensive but she allowed him to help her out of the car.

"Would you like a tour?" he asked once they were inside

"Sure. It's a lovely place. You've been staying here all by yourself?"

"Pretty much. I hired a cleaning service to come in a few times a week and a cook makes meals for me that I can just pop in the oven. Otherwise, I'm pretty much here by myself."

"This is a lot of house for just one man."

"I like my space but I chose this place mainly for the amenities. It has a pool, a hot tub, and a private gym, all of which I make use of. But the selling point of this place is the surprise I'd like to show you. We'll take the tour first and end there if that's all right with you."

"Okay."

Dominic held his hand out to her. Krystina hesitated for a brief moment before taking it. His heart fluttered in his chest at the contact. He proceeded to show her all of the rooms except the one he wanted to keep secret until the time was right. For her part, Krystina complimented what she saw and seemed genuinely interested.

Finally, he led her outside. This was what he wanted her to see. It was a huge garden with manicured shrubs adorned with exotic flowers. The manicured bushes and fruit trees adorned the property in strategic places, forming a maze. There were statues and a bridge over a stream that flowed into a pond surrounded by large stones. As they walked down the man-made trail to the center of the garden, the stones lit up beneath their feet to guide their path.

Krystina gasped. "Dominic, this is so beautiful."

"The most beautiful thing I've ever seen," he said without taking his eyes off her. She might have been referring to the landscaping but Dominic was talking about something entirely different.

"I mean this place is something out of a fantasy world. I wish I would have brought my camera. I'd love to photograph this place."

"You're welcome here at any time, but we should keep going. Our meal is probably getting cold."

Dominic and Krystina kept walking until they reached a table that was decorated with flowers. There were two place settings and a candle in the center. Everything was just as he'd specified. Judging from the look of awe on Krystina's face, she liked the set up as well. He made a mental note to give the staff a bonus the next time he paid them.

She gave him a questioning look. "This is all for me?"

"Yes. I wanted us to have a relaxed night together and talk." He held out a chair for her.

"This place is amazing. Did you buy it or are you renting? If I had the money, I'd buy it for the garden alone," she said still taking in all her surroundings."

"Right now, I'm just renting but the owner is thinking about selling. I've been considering buying a property here so I can have a permanent base when I stay in Spain. It wouldn't be practical to commute from Ibiza when I'm here."

"What is it that's making you consider making a base here?"

"You, of course. Krystina. You didn't think when I go back home this thing will be over between us. I'm in this for the long haul and if that means flying over here every weekend to see you, then so be it. I love you, and even if it makes you uncomfortable to hear it at this point in our relationship, I'm not going to stop telling you how I feel. I bottled my emotions up before and it made me act like a maniac and hurt someone who meant the world to me. You're worth it to me."

She kept her head bowed as if to avoid looking in his eyes.

"Please look at me, Krystina."

When she raised her head, her eyes glistened with the suspicious sheen of tears. "I believe you when you say you love me, Dominic, but I'm terrified."

"I won't ask you why, especially, after all, I've put you through. But I have to know, is there hope?"

"Of course there is because I feel that one day you're going to wake up and regret being with me. Like I told you before, I'm so used to rejection that I've come to expect it. You broke me once and I'm finally picking up the pieces. I'm scared if I let you in, again, and we don't work out, I'll be broken all over again. And the next time, I don't think I'll able to recover." She hastily wiped a tear away.

Hearing her fears about a permanent relationship with him, broke Dominic's heart. He loved this woman to distraction and knowing what he did to her would haunt him for the rest of his life. "Are you hungry?"

His sudden change of subject seemed to throw her off. "Uh, what?" She crinkled her forehead in apparent bewilderment.

"Are you hungry?"

"Just a little."

"On a scale of 1 to 5, where would you say you are right now?"

She shrugged. "About a five, I guess."

He stood up and held out his hand to her. "Come with me."

Krystina wasn't sure what Dominic was up to but his abrupt change of conversation made her question if he was as serious about her as he claimed he was. She took his hand nonetheless and he led her back into the house. He took her to the one room they'd bypassed earlier. She was going to ask him about it but thought it might be some kind of supply closet.

"I wanted to save this for later, but I think what I'm about to show might clear up how I feel about you."

Dominic flipped the light switch on and Krystina gasped in surprise. "Wow, when you wanted me to show you how to take a good picture, I didn't expect anything like this." She inspected the small room which was basically being used as a dark room. There were photos all over the room and mostly of her.

"How did you learn how to develop film like this?" She inspected the pictures one at a time.

"I got a little help from a service. I tried to do it all myself by using the internet but my first few attempts were a disaster. Once I was showed how to do it in person, I got the hang of it. I did this because I remember what you said to me once. Pictures don't lie and I wanted you to see you from my eyes. I'm not as good a photographer as you but I hope you basically get the gist."

One particular wall was covered in pictures of her, mostly taken unawares. These were taken when Krystina thought he was just snapping photos of random scenery. There was a picture of her laughing with one of the local children who was trying to sell her shells from the beach.

There was another of her taking pictures of people passing by. There was another where he'd zoomed in on her face when she'd been in deep thought. He'd managed to not only capture the sadness in her eyes, he had somehow been able to convey the hope for happiness that resided within her.

There was something hauntingly beautiful about the photograph. The other pictures hanging on the wall were clearly done by an amateur but this one looked almost professional. It was true that pictures didn't lie but it was almost correct that a good photographer could convey their own feelings through a picture. It looked as if this picture was taken by someone who loved her.

Krystina didn't realize she was crying until she tasted a salty tear in the corner of her mouth. "Dominic…you took this?"

Dominic moved behind her and put his hands on her shoulders. "I know they're not as good as yours but I was hoping you would see what I'm trying to get at."

"You really do love me," she whispered.

"Yes, and I'll keep telling it to you until the day I die." Gently, he turned her around to face him. "Stop me now, Krystina because I'm going to kiss you."

Her lips quivered and she looked into his eyes. Life was full of uncertainties but the one thing she knew right then and there was that she was tired of being scared. She was ready to fully give herself over to him. Krystina wanted her happy ending but she realized she wouldn't have it without him. "I want this."

"Once I start, I may not be able to stop," he warned with a low growl.

"Maybe, I don't want you to." She tilted her head back to receive his kiss.

With a growl, he lowered his head and covered her lips with his. Krystina wrapped her arms around his neck, returning his kiss and matching his hunger. How had she gone so long without his touch and how did she think she could exist without it. Perhaps, she and Dominic had been destined to be together from the beginning of time and both were too stubborn to admit it, but being in his arms again, Krystina felt whole.

Dominic cupped her bottom in his large palms and pulled her against his pelvis. She felt the thickness of his erection poking through his slacks. He grinded against her as his kiss became more persistent. As he slipped his tongue into her mouth, she threaded her fingers through his hair.

Their tongues dancing, and dueling, tasting and licking, exploring and loving.

Finally, Krystina turned her head away to catch her breath.

Dominic buried his face against her neck and rained kisses all over her bare skin. "Oh, duchess, you have no idea how much I want you like this." He lifted Krystina off her feet and she instinctively wrapped her legs around his waist and arms around his neck.

"Hold on tight, duchess, because I'm going to make love to you, so you'd better make your objections now or hold your peace."

Her heart swelled with so much love for this man that she could barely speak. There was nothing freer than finally letting go of the hurt, pain, and shame to love openly. Krystina's response was to press her lips to his.

"I love you," Dominic murmured against her lips before carrying her out of the room and down the hall to his bedroom.

Once there, he gently returned Krystina to her feet and proceeded to unzip her dress. When it pooled at her feet, she stepped out of the article of clothing and moved her arms up to unhook her strapless bras. Dominic captured her hands. "No. Let me."

With a shiver, Krystina obeyed his soft command. Instead of removing her bra right away, he placed more kisses on her exposed skin starting at the shell of her ears and then moving to her neck. He then placed kisses on her chest and knelt to press his lips against her belly.

She had to admit that she liked it when Dominic was rough but she found that she liked it just as much when he was gentle. Still, on his knees, he reached up and unfastened her bra before sliding her panties down her legs.

"Hold on to me, duchess," he said with a throaty command before lifting one of her legs and putting it over his shoulders. She held on tight as he latched on to her pussy like a man starving. He sucked on her labia before slipping two fingers inside her channel.

"You're already so wet and ready for me. Did you miss my mouth on you, duchess?"

"Yes."

He smiled. "Good, because I missed the taste of you." Dominic buried his face against her womanhood exploring every inch of her with his tongue, running it from the top of her slit to the crack of her ass. Her knees grew wobblier with each stroke and every time his finger plowed into her, she made it closer to nirvana.

"Oh, God, Dominic, I'm going to come…but I want you inside of me when it happens."

With one long slurp of her pussy, he raised his head. "Is that what you really want, duchess?"

"Yes. Make love to me."

He gently put her foot back on the floor before rising. When he started to undress, she shook her head. "No. Let me."

Dominic's response was a low groan.

As she removed each article of his clothing, she ran her fingertips along the expanse of his exposed skin until he was as naked as she. His thick cock jutted forward, ready for action. "You have a beautiful body," she whispered, circling his cock in her hand.

"Oh, duchess. You have no idea what you're doing to me."

She giggled. "I think I might have a small one."

"Mmm, if you keep touching me like that, I'm not going to be able to hold out much longer." He gripped her by the wrist and pulled her against him before covering her mouth with a hungry kiss.

Slowly, he guided her to the bed where he collapsed on top of her. With their mouths still merged, Dominic nudged her legs apart with his knee. He then guided himself to her entrance.

Raising his head, he looked deep into her eyes. "I love you, duchess. I always have. And, I always will." Dominic entered her with one powerful thrust.

Krystina had missed the feel of being so deliciously stretched by his thickness. She nearly wept with joy as he slowly moved in and out of her. Being with him like this, it was hard to imagine that they were once enemies. Their heads might have resisted what was always meant to be, but their hearts always knew.

Their hands intertwined together as Dominic moved deeper with each thrust. She raised her hips, matching his rhythm as they moved together. Every one of her senses was engaged in this act of love-making. His scent was driving her absolutely mad; combined with the sound of his saying her name over again, the taste of his lips on hers, the feel of their bodies sliding together in perfect harmony and the sight of the man taking her body to heights she never thought she'd achieve, sent her hurtling into an explosive orgasm. She screamed until her throat was raw.

The sex between them had been hot before but this was special. Each had given their all.

Dominic gritted his teeth and shuddered against her as he shortly reached completion after her.

They held each other each tight not saying anything while they both came down from their high. Dominic stroked the side of her face. "Love you, so much. I promise I'll spend the rest of my life proving that to you."

She raised her head. "Dominic? Where do we go from here? I signed a contract with Sandoval. I can't get out of it for another year."

He kissed the top of her head. "It doesn't matter where we are in the world. We'll make time for each other. There's this invention called airplanes. I hear they fly transatlantic," he teased.

Krystina popped his chest playfully. "Be serious."

Dominic grinned. "What? I can't joke with my lady?"

"Of course you can. But I'm just nervous. I'll be in Madrid, and you have to go back to New York."

He captured her chin between his forefinger and thumb. "Krystina, look at me."

She raised her lids to meet his gaze. "Do you love me?"

"Yes," she said without hesitation.

"And I love you. And I promise we will be together. I waited a lifetime for you even when I didn't realize it. I'm not letting you go and I'm certainly not going to allow distance to get in the way. I once said to you, that I own you. But the truth is, you own me. Heart, body and soul."

And with that, Dominic pressed his lips against hers.

Epilogue

Krystina was full of nervous energy as her plane landed. She was finally coming home. The last time she returned after living overseas, it had been with a completely different feeling. This time there was no apprehension or fear. The ghosts of the past had finally been laid to rest.

For the past year, she fulfilled her contract with the Sandoval Group. Tomas had been very understanding when she'd handed in her resignation. Even though they no longer dated, they remained friends.

Krystina had enjoyed her time in Madrid, but the best part of living there had been experiencing it with Dominic, who had kept his word about doing everything in his power to make things work out. Every other weekend, he would fly out to see her and they would make the most of their time together.

One her birthday, Dominic had gifted her the villa with the magical garden to do with as she willed. It was nice to know that she'd always have a base in Europe whenever she got the traveling bug. Poppy and Felix had already claimed it as their vacation spot. Just as she imagined, her new property had been a dream to photograph. In her spare time, she'd taken pictures of it and had even paid a few of the locals to pose in it for her.

Dominic had suggested that she make a photo book and send it out to studios and magazines looking for professional photographers. With his encouragement, she'd done just that, so now she wasn't just going back home for Dominic, she'd be working for a magazine as an associate photographer. She enjoyed her last two jobs, but her heart wasn't completely in it. Now, she would be living her passion with a man she loved by her side.

Her heart beat wildly in her chest as she thought of Dominic. It was truly a pleasure to be his. He was thoughtful, had a great sense of humor and was the most considerate and passionate lover. Sometimes, he was rough with hair pulling and spanking making her scream until she lost her voice. And then other times, he'd make love to her so gently, she wept from the tenderness of his touch.

A couple years ago, if someone would have told her that her biggest enemy would be the greatest love of her life, she would have laughed. But, that was what Dominic had become to her.

Once the flight attendant opened the door of the plane, Krystina couldn't get off fast enough. She impatiently waited for the passengers to get off before her and when it was finally her turn, she practically raced down the walkway to get her baggage. Dominic had let her know that someone would be waiting for her at the airport.

She tapped her foot on the escalator, eager to get her bags. By the time she reached the bottom, she saw a man in a black suit holding a large sign with her name on it. *Ms. Krystina Jackson.*

As she drew near, the scent of his cologne was a dead giveaway. "Dominic!"

He lowered the sign with a huge grin. "Hey, duchess. How was your flight?"

"Who cares?" She said before launching herself into his arms and pressing kisses all over his face.

"Whoa, if I would have known I'd get this type of greeting, I'd make you go overseas all the time," he teased.

"You'd miss me too much."

"Damn right. I would." He covered her mouth with a hungry kiss which she returned enthusiastically. Krystina pressed her body against his. It had only been a few weeks since she'd last seen him but any time away from Dominic was an eternity.

"Eww, you two. Get a room." Poppy interrupted them.

Krystina pulled away with a laugh and was delighted to not only see Poppy but Felix and Uncle Charles. "You all came!" She wrapped her arms around Poppy and gave her a tight squeeze.

Felix grinned walking up to her. "We wanted to give you a proper welcome." He draped his arm around her and gave her a hug.

"What about me, my dear. Do I get a hug?" Uncle Charles lumbered forward.

She walked into his arms and gave him a huge hug. "I missed you, too."

"Promise me, you won't go away so long, again. I don't think this old heart can take it."

"And I don't think Dominic will let me, either." Krystina giggled.

Dominic pulled her to his side. "Damn right. From now on, wherever I go, you go." He dropped a kiss on the top of her head. "All right, let's go get your bag. I promised this lot we'd go somewhere special for dinner."

Krystina didn't think she could possibly get any happier. She was reunited with her family and the man she loved. She'd found her happily ever after.

Dominic's heart skipped several beats when he saw his beautiful woman come down the escalator. The best part was seeing her gorgeous smile. And it was just for him.

This past year of their long distance romance had been torture every time they had to say goodbye. But now that she was home, he vowed to spend the rest of his days making her happy. Once her baggage was loaded in the car, Dominic patted the side of his pants pocket to ensure the ring box was still there. Not only would the family be celebrating Krystina's homecoming at dinner, but something else as well. Something big. Tonight was going to be special.

About the Author

NYT and USA Today Bestselling Author Eve has always enjoyed creating characters and stories from an early age. As a child she was always getting into mischief, so when she lost her television privileges (which was often), writing was her outlet. Her stories have gotten quite a bit spicier since then! When she's not writing or spending time with her family, Eve is reading, baking, traveling or kicking butt in 80's trivia. She loves hearing from her readers. She can be contacted through her website at: www.evevaughn.com.

More Books From Eve Vaughn:

Finding Divine

Whatever He Wants

Jilted

Relentless

Run

The Auction

Dirty

The Kyriakis Curse:
Book One of the Kyriakis Series

GianMarco:
Book One of the Blood Brothers Series

Niccolo:
Book Two of the Blood Brothers Series

Romeo:
Book Three of the Blood Brothers Series

Jagger:
Book Four of the Blood Brothers Series

Made in United States
Orlando, FL
23 March 2022